HOT TOPICS

THE DEATH PENALTY
JUST PUNISHMENT OR CRUEL PRACTICE?

By Allison Krumsiek

Portions of this book originally appeared in *Death Penalty* by Syd Golston.

Published in 2018 by
Lucent Press, an Imprint of Greenhaven Publishing, LLC
353 3rd Avenue
Suite 255
New York, NY 10010

Copyright © 2018 Greenhaven Press, a part of Gale, Cengage Learning
Gale and Greenhaven Press are registered trademarks used herein under license.

All new materials copyright © 2018 Lucent Press, an Imprint of Greenhaven Publishing, LLC.

All rights reserved. No part of this book may be reproduced in any form without permission in writing from the publisher, except by a reviewer.

Designer: Deanna Paternostro
Editor: Jessica Moore

Library of Congress Cataloging-in-Publication Data

Names: Krumsiek, Allison, author.
Title: Death penalty : just punishment or cruel practice? / Allison Krumsiek.
Description: First Edition. | New York : Lucent Press, [2018] | Series: Hot topics | Includes bibliographical references and index.
Identifiers: LCCN 2017043590| ISBN 9781534562936 (pbk. book) | ISBN 9781534562059 (library bound book) | ISBN 9781534562066 (eBook)
Subjects: LCSH: Capital punishment–Juvenile literature.
Classification: LCC HV8694 .K78 2018 | DDC 364.66–dc23
LC record available at https://lccn.loc.gov/2017043590

CPSIA compliance information: Batch #CW18KL: For further information contact Greenhaven Publishing LLC, New York, New York at 1-844-317-7404.

Please visit our website, www.greenhavenpublishing.com. For a free color catalog of all our high-quality books, call toll free 1-844-317-7404 or fax 1-844-317-7405.

CONTENTS

FOREWORD	4
INTRODUCTION	6
"An Eye for an Eye"	
CHAPTER 1	11
Sanctioning Punishment	
CHAPTER 2	27
Support for the Death Penalty	
CHAPTER 3	41
The Case Against the Death Penalty	
CHAPTER 4	59
The Court's Rule on Capital Punishment	
CHAPTER 5	75
A Global Look at the Death Penalty	
NOTES	88
DISCUSSION QUESTIONS	92
ORGANIZATIONS TO CONTACT	94
FOR MORE INFORMATION	96
INDEX	98
PICTURE CREDITS	103
ABOUT THE AUTHOR	104

FOREWORD

Adolescence is a time when many people begin to take notice of the world around them. News channels, blogs, and talk radio shows are constantly promoting one view or another; very few are unbiased. Young people also hear conflicting information from parents, friends, teachers, and acquaintances. Often, they will hear only one side of an issue or be given flawed information. People who are trying to support a particular viewpoint may cite inaccurate facts and statistics on their blogs, and news programs present many conflicting views of important issues in our society. In a world where it seems everyone has a platform to share their thoughts, it can be difficult to find unbiased, accurate information about important issues.

It is not only facts that are important. In blog posts, in comments on online videos, and on talk shows, people will share opinions that are not necessarily true or false, but can still have a strong impact. For example, many young people struggle with their body image. Seeing or hearing negative comments about particular body types online can have a huge effect on the way someone views himself or herself and may lead to depression and anxiety. Although it is important not to keep information hidden from young people under the guise of protecting them, it is equally important to offer encouragement on issues that affect their mental health.

The titles in the Hot Topics series provide readers with different viewpoints on important issues in today's society. Many of these issues, such as teen pregnancy and Internet safety, are of immediate concern to young people. This series aims to give readers factual context on these crucial topics in a way that lets them form their own opinions. The facts presented throughout also serve to empower readers to help themselves or support people they know who are struggling with many of the challenges adolescents face today. Although negative viewpoints are not ignored or downplayed, this series allows young people to see that the challenges they face are not insurmountable. Eating disorders can be overcome, the Internet can be navigated safely, and pregnant teens do not have to feel hopeless.

Quotes encompassing all viewpoints are presented and cited so readers can trace them back to their original source, verifying for themselves whether the information comes from a reputable place. Additional books and websites are listed, giving readers a starting point from which to continue their own research. Chapter questions encourage discussion, allowing young people to hear and understand their classmates' points of view as they further solidify their own. Full-color photographs and enlightening charts provide a deeper understanding of the topics at hand. All of these features augment the informative text, helping young people understand the world they live in and formulate their own opinions concerning the best way they can improve it.

"An Eye for an Eye"

Since the dawn of civilization, societies have sought to punish criminals. For especially severe crimes, such as murder, many societies have used death as punishment. Capital punishment, the penalty of death for those judged guilty of certain extreme crimes, is as old as the earliest written history. For almost 4,000 years, the death penalty has been carried out—and argued over—in societies throughout the world.

From ancient times to today, societies have questioned whether the death penalty is justified. Who decides which crimes are so severe that the guilty must be executed? Does fear of the death penalty discourage people who might commit such acts? Can a community's desire for revenge justify executions, or does that revenge make society itself more brutal? Human beings make mistakes—what if an innocent person is put to death?

Early Greeks and Romans were less concerned about the justification of the death penalty and instead focused more on how it would be applied among the different classes; laws were different for nobles, commoners, and slaves. The Athenian lawgiver Draco believed that even minor infractions deserved execution, and for about 25 years, death was the penalty for all crimes in Athens. The Romans used methods of utmost cruelty: Depending on social status, criminals were beaten, stoned, drowned, buried alive, or crucified.

Beginning in the Middle Ages, England witnessed extremes of opinion toward capital punishment. Some began to question the morality of taking a life for a life, and William the Conqueror, the first king of England, outlawed it altogether. The English death penalty was later restored and heavily enforced, often in the form of beheading for nobles and hanging for commoners—the word "capital" in capital punishment is derived from *capitalis*, Latin for "of the head." By the 1700s, the English courts had punished 222 crimes with death. These crimes included murder and kidnapping as well as minor crimes such as stealing or cutting down a neighbor's trees.

Capital punishment laws in the North American colonies reflected their British heritage. The first colonial execution was carried out at Jamestown in 1608, when George Kendall, who was accused of spying for Spain, was found guilty of treason against the settlement and hanged. Each colony developed its own criminal code that required capital punishment for many crimes, including murder, conspiracy, and blasphemy. Witchcraft was also punishable by death—the notorious Salem witchcraft trials of 1692 resulted in the hangings of 19 innocent women and men.

The 18th-century Age of Reason in Europe produced a generation of philosophers who opposed the death penalty, and their writings affected the thinking of citizens in both the Old World and the New. One of these reflections appeared in *On Crimes and Punishments*, originally published in 1764 by Cesare Beccaria, an Italian judge who claimed that capital punishment was neither necessary nor useful. He termed it "a war of a whole nation against a citizen."[1] Beccaria thought execution was necessary only if the death of the accused could ensure the safety of the whole nation. Thomas Jefferson had read Beccaria and the other philosophers who wished to reform the criminal codes. He proposed a revision of the laws of Virginia to recommend the death penalty only for treason and murder. Jefferson's attempt was defeated in Virginia's House of Burgesses by just one vote; many legislators had shared his views.

Physician Benjamin Rush of Pennsylvania was even more opposed to capital punishment than Jefferson. He was one of the first to argue that it had a brutalization effect upon society, which would actually encourage more violence among citizens rather than prevent it. At the urging of Rush and Benjamin Franklin, Pennsylvania repealed the death penalty in 1794 for all offenses except first-degree murder (murder that is intentional and premeditated).

Many states limited capital punishment in the 19th century. Judges and juries had to examine each capital case individually to decide whether death would be imposed. Public hangings ceased; after the invention of electricity, some states switched to the electric chair, or later the gas chamber, both of which were considered more humane.

In the 1800s, juries and judges had to decide whether death would be imposed in each case. Lady Justice, shown here, symbolizes fair and balanced administration of the law.

In the 20th century, public opinion for and against the death penalty changed depending on current events. Nine states abolished capital punishment between 1895 and 1917.

However, after the Russian Revolution in 1917, Americans feared similar revolution and socialism would spread to the United States, and the death penalty became popular once again. Most states resumed executions as a general state of suspicion spread over the country.

Intense feelings against executions erupted again when two Italian American anarchists (someone who is against any ruling power or authority), Nicola Sacco and Bartolomeo Vanzetti, were executed for robbery and murder on August 23, 1927. More than 250,000 people gathered in Boston to protest their death, and in 1977, the governor of Massachusetts stated that no stigma should be associated with them and that they had not been treated fairly. Criminologists wrote that capital punishment was a necessary social control during the Great Depression of the 1930s, when unemployment and desperation threatened to unravel society.

Campaigns to end the death penalty across the United States were met with resistance. In 1972, opponents of capital punishment brought the case of *Furman v. Georgia* to the Supreme Court. In a 5–4 decision, the justices ruled that the death penalty as it was then enforced by the states violated the Eighth Amendment against cruel and unusual punishment, and all death row executions ceased. In 1976, the Court reversed itself in the case of *Gregg v. Georgia*, recognizing newer and fairer criminal codes and sentencing policies. Executions began again as some states adopted lethal injection, which was considered the least painful or violent method.

Support for the death penalty has declined since 1972 as the number of executions in the United States has also steadily declined. Supporters of the death penalty remain steadfast, though. Studies disagree over whether it deters criminals, but many Americans still believe in the principles of the Code of Hammurabi and of the Bible: "an eye for an eye." Many still support the death penalty as punishment for the most horrible of crimes.

Other Americans oppose capital punishment on many grounds. They cite the old Enlightenment philosophies about unfairness, failure to prevent crime, and the evils of executing the wrong person. They note that more than two-thirds of all countries have abolished capital punishment, including most of the advanced industrial countries.

Protests have centered on the methods of execution as well as its use in general. The Supreme Court heard oral arguments for and against the use of lethal injection on January 7, 2008, in the Kentucky case of *Baze v. Rees*, and the justices' decision denied that the practice of lethal injection comprised cruel and unusual punishment, permitting the continuation of executions in the states. In 2014's *Glossip v. Gross*, the Supreme Court ruled that it was the prisoners who must prove that lethal injection is cruel and unusual, not the state. In 2017, protestors against the death penalty in Ohio stated that the death penalty was used inconsistently and was expensive for the state. They added that these prisoners could sometimes be waiting 20 years for the death penalty sentence to actually be carried out.

Internationally, nations such as China, Iran, Saudi Arabia, and Pakistan join the United States in filling the world's death rows. At the same time, member countries of the European Union have abolished the death penalty. Organizations such as the United Nations and Amnesty International work against capital punishment around the world.

Sanctioning Punishment

Capital punishment has been used to punish criminals since the beginning of recorded history. Laws determining who might receive the death penalty have changed over time and across nations. Today, many nations have abolished the death penalty, although some, including the United States, continue to execute people.

The Earliest Laws

"An eye for an eye and a tooth for a tooth." This saying appears in the Code of Hammurabi and in the Bible and is still used today. The Book of Leviticus contains the most direct reference to a civil death penalty in this divine proclamation to Moses: "Anyone who takes the life of a human being is to be put to death … Anyone who injures their neighbor is to be injured in the same manner: fracture for fracture, eye for eye, tooth for tooth. The one who has inflicted the injury must suffer the same injury."[2] In Western cultures, that concept of equal retribution for taking a life became the basis for thousands of years of public policy on capital punishment.

The Old Testament prescribes the penalty of death for dozens of misdeeds other than murder. Many of these seem like minor offenses for such an extreme punishment: trying to convert an Israelite to another religion, attempting to communicate with the dead, adultery, and even cursing at one's parents. A common execution method described in the Bible is death by stoning. In reality, few were executed because the standards of proof were so high. Even a murder verdict required two eyewitnesses.

Biblical scholars are careful to point out that this advice was given to the Israelites as a society, not to individuals who would create mayhem by carrying out their personal revenge. It was perhaps the first societal policy that can be traced in the ancient world, although some evidence suggests that the Chinese had law codes that included capital punishment before 2500 BC.

Stoning was an early form of capital punishment.

The Babylonian Code of Hammurabi from around 1750 BC is the first dated evidence of a state's statutory use of the death penalty. Citizens of ancient Babylon gathered in the city's public square to stare at an 8-foot-tall (2.4 m) column of black stone, carved on all its sides with writing. Those who could read the words on the column pronounced for the crowd the 282 laws of the kingdom, proclaimed by Hammurabi, ruler of Babylon. Many of the laws address crimes and their consequences, which call for equal and direct revenge. Law 229 of the code reads: "If a builder has built a house for a man, and has not made his work sound, and the house he built has fallen and caused the death of its owner, that builder shall be put to death."[3]

Along with causing another's death, many sexual acts were considered capital crimes in Babylon. Thefts from the royal treasury, selling stolen goods, kidnapping, hiding a fugitive slave, and disorderly conduct in a tavern were also considered capital crimes. In all, there were 25 laws in the code that called for the death penalty. Certain offenses called for specific methods of execution; those who committed adultery were drowned, and burglars were hanged at the scene of the crime.

Capital punishment also existed in ancient China, according to the writings of Confucius and his followers. Confucians believed more in the power of the virtuous example to deter criminal behavior than in the sanction of punishment, but they also recognized the occasional justification for the death penalty. They opposed the more barbaric death penalties of the time, which included sawing someone in half.

The Greeks in Homer's time, around ninth or eighth century BC, acted upon the urge for retaliation for a homicide. The victim's family caught and killed the murderer or accepted a blood price—a payment for the death that would restore peace and satisfy the aggrieved family.

Draco's Code in ancient Athens, recorded in 621 BC, punished even trivial crimes with death and is the source of the term "draconian," which means "overly severe." It was

The Code of Hammurabi consisted of 282 laws, 25 of which resulted in death if they were broken.

said that Draco's laws were written in blood rather than ink. The civil laws were also intolerably strict, such as the punishment of enslavement for nonpayment of debts.

Around 20 years after the Athenian leader Solon replaced Draco, a much more lenient system emerged that prescribed the death penalty only for crimes that endangered the entire community and offered permanent banishment from Athens to defendants who admitted their guilt. These Athenian statutes remained in place with few changes for more than 200 years. They were carried out in a hierarchy of justice courts, set up to try different degrees of crimes, including a separate court for repeat killers. Aristotle wrote that those repeat offenders had to defend themselves from a boat so they would not contaminate the members of the court, who were seated at the water's edge.

The Gadfly of Athens

The Athenian philosopher Socrates was known as "the gadfly of Athens" because he constantly reminded the state of its proper duties; some saw this as an annoyance, like a fly that constantly bites a horse. He questioned the ancestral gods and the process of democracy itself, claiming that in no other craft would the craftsmen be chosen by popular vote. His ideas about virtue challenged the concept of the will of the gods.

Socrates's disciples included Alcibiades and Critias, both of whom betrayed Athenian democracy in favor of its enemy Sparta, and this association led many to think that the philosopher's influence on young leaders threatened the state.

Socrates was accused of corrupting the youth of Athens and disbelieving in the gods. A jury of around 500 freeborn male citizen volunteers, selected by lottery, was called to decide the case; a guilty verdict required only a majority of the jurors. Socrates was condemned by just over half the jury.

After their first verdict, a second was called to decide Socrates's penalty. The prosecutor asked for death, and

SANCTIONING PUNISHMENT   15

The most famous of all Athenian trials resulted in the execution of the philosopher Socrates in 399 BC.

The Romans' Law of the Twelve Tables named capital punishment for several crimes, most of them forms of murder, including poisoning and assassination. Murder within the family was punished most cruelly. The later *lex Cornelia* (Cornelian Law) said that "he who *killed* a father or mother, grandfather or grandmother was punished ... by being whipped till he bled, sewn up in a sack, with a dog, a [rooster], a viper, and an ape, and thrown into the sea."[4]

Slaves and foreigners under the Romans suffered at the hands of the law more severely than Roman citizens. A slave could be tortured, for instance. Execution by crucifixion was reserved for noncitizens who had committed the worst crimes; the

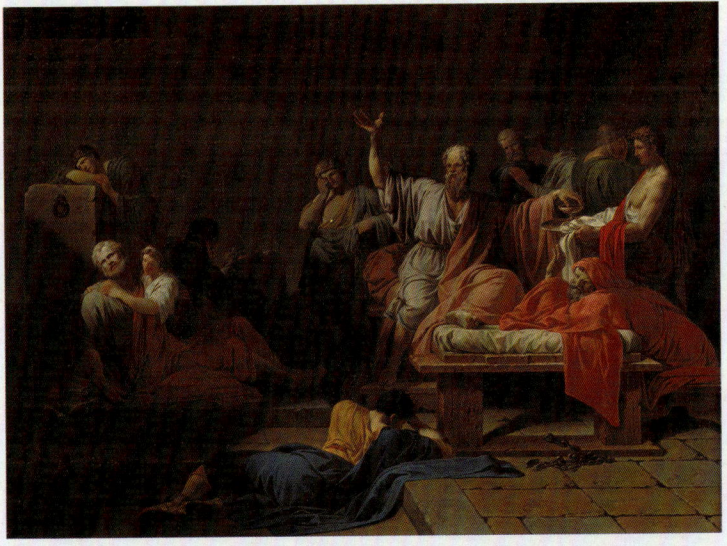

the jury agreed. In accordance with his long-held ideas of obeying the law, the philosopher carried out his execution by his own hand, drinking a bowl of hemlock, which killed him.

Socrates is shown here drinking hemlock as punishment in the painting The Death of Socrates *by Jean-François-Pierre Peyron.*

crucifixion process included whipping and carrying the cross to the site of execution. Victims who were nailed to the cross actually died of asphyxiation, or suffocation, while those who were tied to it died of starvation, some surviving as long as nine days.

The Islamic laws of the Qur'an were recorded in the seventh century AD and included capital punishment for many crimes, including robbery, adultery, and religious crimes. Oddly, murder was not mentioned among them; murder was to be treated as a civil crime between families and decided by the relatives of the victim, who could choose death or retribution payment.

BASIC HUMAN RIGHTS

"All people have the right to life, and we all have the right to be free from cruel, inhuman, and degrading punishment. These are human rights that people have, regardless of whether they have been convicted of crimes."

—Amnesty International, a global group that demands equal human rights for all people

"Death Penalty," Amnesty International, accessed September 14, 2017, www.amnestyusa.org/issues/death-penalty/.

Heretics and Revolutions: The Middle Ages

Roman Catholic Christianity became the most important institution in Europe in the Middle Ages—from around the fifth to the fifteenth century AD. In medieval European societies, the death penalty was often inflicted for violations of faith, and church officials decided what qualified as a violation of faith. The laws of this era provided for the execution of suspected witches, sorcerers, nonbelievers, and heretics (those who did not conform to the official teachings of the church). The Cathars in France and the Hussites in the Czech region were burned at the stake for their contrary religious beliefs.

The most famous heretic to suffer this fate was Joan of Arc, a teenage peasant who claimed that visions of the saints called her to lead the French army and drive the English from France during the Hundred Years' War. Dressed in men's armor, Joan led the French triumphantly at Orléans in 1429. The English captured her just a year later and tried her as a heretic.

Clergy who supported the English found Joan guilty of claiming false divine revelations, of immodesty in wearing male clothes, and even of making incorrect claims that the saints spoke French rather than English. On May 30, 1431, Joan was tied to a pillar in the marketplace of Rouen. Holding a small wooden cross, she called the names of her saints as the flames grew higher. According to the legend of Joan of Arc, her organs were found in the ashes, which were then burned two more times.

In the later Middle Ages, the Catholic Church set up Inquisition bodies in several states, intended to root out heresy and execute people who refused to repent; the most violent of these was the Spanish Inquisition. Tomás de Torquemada, the Spanish grand inquisitor, was infamous for the use of torture to convert heretics, but thousands of prisoners resisted such tactics and were burned at the stake.

In this artist's rendering, Joan of Arc is shown being executed by burning at the stake.

Protestants were just as likely to put their religious enemies to death. During Henry VIII's reign, 72,000 people were executed. When Henry broke with Rome, he founded his own Anglican church and seized monasteries all over England. Catholics in

Revolution and State Executions

The most infamous executions in history took place in Paris during 10 months of the French Revolution that are called the "Reign of Terror." Between 18,000 and 40,000 people died, mostly in ghastly and crowded public spectacles.

The French Revolution began in 1789 as a movement to wrest power from the court of King Louis XVI and place it in the hands of an elected national assembly. Immediate violence erupted; in Paris, ordinary citizens attacked the Bastille fortress to get their hands on firearms, and in the countryside, peasants revolted and stormed the manors of their landlords.

Louis XVI was tried for crimes against the people of France and beheaded by the guillotine in January 1793. Members of the radical Jacobin political party, under their extremist leader Maximilien Robespierre, formed a Committee of Public Safety and began to eliminate their enemies.

Queen Marie Antoinette was found guilty of treason and was paraded in an open cart through the streets of Paris to her beheading. Thousands shared her fate during the Reign of Terror, with arrests, trials, and executions orchestrated by Robespierre. Anyone suspected of opposing the revolution was swiftly tried and sent to the guillotine. In a final reaction to the horrific violence, legislators turned on Robespierre himself. On July 27, 1794, Robespierre and 21 of his followers were guillotined.

The guillotine was introduced in 1792 and was largely used during the Reign of Terror.

the north of England protested the seizures in what was known as the Pilgrimage of Grace. Henry received the protesters, heard their petitions, and sent them home—where they were arrested, tried for treason, and hanged. Reginald Pole, the last Catholic archbishop of Canterbury, wrote to Henry, "Thy butcheries and horrible executions have made England the slaughter house of innocence."[5]

Punishment in the 1700s

Executions for common crimes in Europe were abundant in the 17th and 18th centuries. By the 1700s, 222 crimes were punishable by death, including stealing a sheep, cutting down a tree, and robbing a rabbit warren. Eventually, many judges considered death penalties for such crimes excessive, and other penalties came into use. The justices commuted, or changed, sentences to imprisonment and deportation, often to English prison colonies in Australia and the American colony of Georgia.

For centuries, a prisoner could escape the gallows through "benefit of clergy." If they could prove that they were a member of the church—a priest, a monk, or even a non-ordained cleric—they could be set free. The only way to know for certain that the defendant was indeed a member of a religious order was to ask them to read out loud, as churchmen were the only literate members of society. If the defendant read from the Bible successfully, they were spared.

The 18th-century philosophical movement called the Enlightenment brought about a questioning of the traditional values of the Middle Ages, replacing tradition with human reason as the arbiter of right and wrong in society. Optimism and reform replaced fear and punishment in western Europe, as well as in the English colonies. Philosophers, such as Jean-Jacques Rousseau, Voltaire, and Denis Diderot in France; John Locke, Jeremy Bentham, and David Hume in England; and Thomas Jefferson, Thomas Paine, and Benjamin Franklin in the colonies, began to challenge the value and the morality of capital punishment.

Cesare Beccaria, born into a noble family in Milan in 1738, published his treatise called *On Crimes and Punishments* in 1764.

Beccaria rejected the death penalty's ability to deter criminals, believing that life imprisonment was more dreaded by the populace. He wrote that a society brutalized itself by inflicting capital punishment: "The punishment of death is pernicious to society, from the example of barbarity it affords ... Is it not absurd, that the laws, which detest and punish homicide, should, in order to prevent murder, publicly commit murder themselves?"[6] Beccaria recognized only one situation in which capital punishment was appropriate: when the criminal, although deprived of their liberty and imprisoned, still has the power and connections to upset a nation's security and start a revolution.

The Influence of the Enlightenment

Most European nations and the United States built larger prisons in the early 19th century and reduced the number of capital crimes and the number of actual executions. England's 222 capital crimes were reduced by nearly half. Public executions, formerly thought to serve as a deterrent to future criminals, were attacked as grisly spectacles and occasions of drunkenness, fighting, and obscenity. The last public execution, of Rainey Bethea for the crime of rape, drew a mob of 20,000 onlookers in 1936. Public executions were replaced by executions in prisons.

Michigan was the first state to end the death penalty for all crimes except treason, followed by Rhode Island and Wisconsin. When states that kept capital punishment got rid of mandatory sentences, people considered it a great reform step forward: Judges would decide, based on specific circumstances of a crime, whether it warranted the extreme punishment.

However, most states kept the death penalty and used it. Southern states increased the number of capital crimes, especially those committed by slaves. Slave uprisings in the 1820s and 1830s resulted in large-scale executions. Some states continued to use capital punishment outside of the court system. Lynching, which is when a mass mob decides that a death penalty applies and enforces the punishment themselves, occurred throughout the United States from 1882 to 1968. African American men and women were pursued by mobs of citizens, hanged, and burned, and their bodies were left as warnings to others. Some of these people were accused of crimes, but the majority of lynchings were based on racism.

Death penalty reformers often supported the abolition of slavery as well, and until the end of the American Civil War and the Reconstruction period after it, reform energy was spent on getting rid of slavery and not on capital punishment issues. By the turn of the 20th century, prison and sentencing reform were back on the agenda.

Electrocution replaced hanging and firing squads as the method of execution in many states after demonstrations by Thomas Edison on the power of electricity to kill. Edison wanted to show that his method of creating electricity was safer than his rival George Westinghouse's alternating current. Edison eventually convinced the state of New York that the Westinghouse method could be used for capital punishment. The first criminal to die in the electric chair was

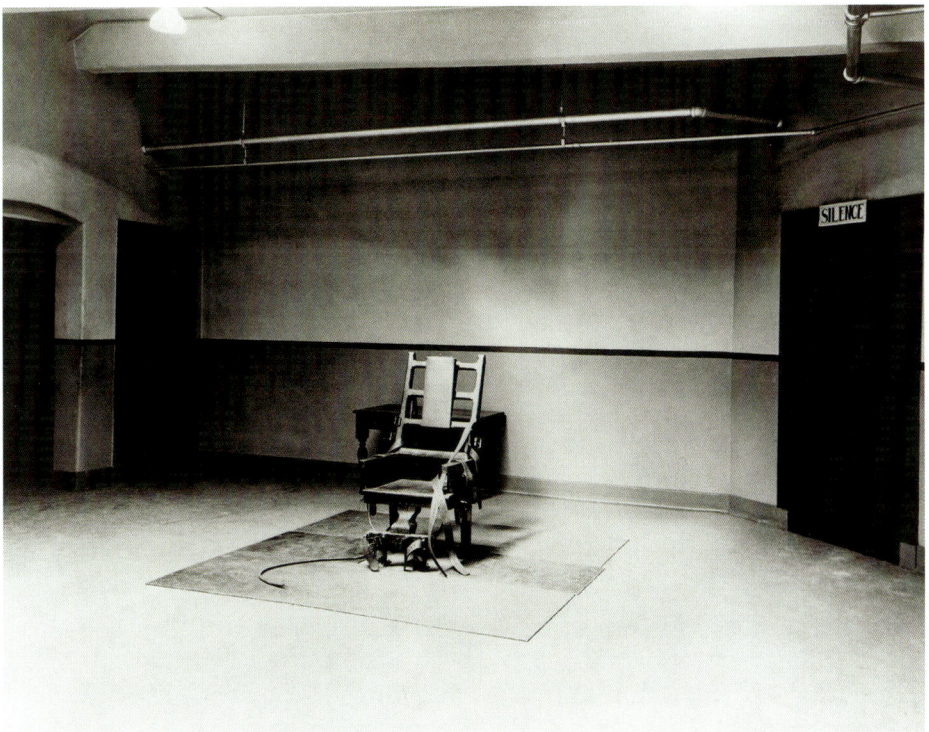

The electric chair, one of which is shown here, was a popular method of execution from the late 19th century to the mid-20th century.

William Kemmler, executed in 1890 in New York. The execution was disturbing and produced a startling display of effects that caused the prison doctor to declare that there would never be another electrocution. However, his prediction was wrong.

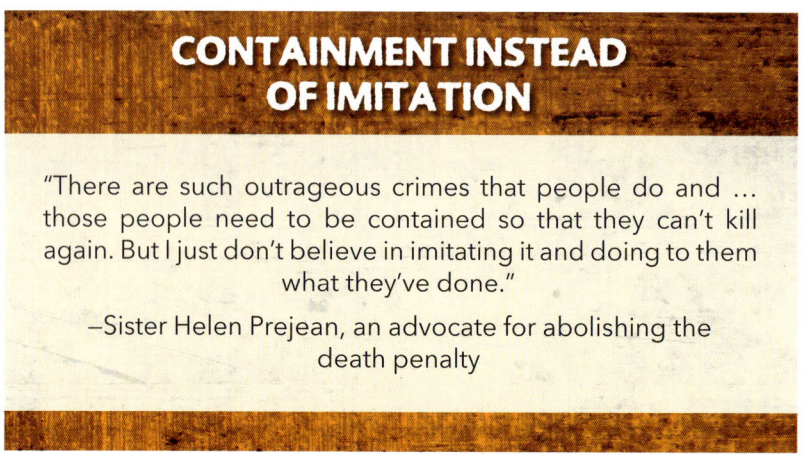

CONTAINMENT INSTEAD OF IMITATION

"There are such outrageous crimes that people do and … those people need to be contained so that they can't kill again. But I just don't believe in imitating it and doing to them what they've done."

—Sister Helen Prejean, an advocate for abolishing the death penalty

"Sister Helen Prejean Interview," PBS *Frontline*, accessed September 14, 2017. www.pbs.org/wgbh/pages/frontline/angel/interviews/hprejean.html.

American Support Declines

The reformers' efforts returned with the Progressive Era—from 1890 until 1920. Capital punishment reform joined a long list of movements that aimed to improve American society, including labor unions, women's suffrage, slum clearance, prohibition of alcohol, and cleaning up political corruption. At the outbreak of World War I and the Russian Revolution of 1917, fear of class conflict and radical immigrants changed attitudes toward capital punishment, which returned in most of the states that had abolished it during the early years of the Progressive Era.

An average of 167 executions per year occurred during the Great Depression of the 1930s, which was more than at any other decade in American history. Many feared that the American capitalist system itself might be overthrown unless the poor, the unemployed, and their radical champions—the left-wing Socialists and Communists—were controlled and punished by vigilant authorities.

Innocent and Executed

On April 15, 1920, two paymasters from a factory in South Braintree, Massachusetts, were gunned down and more than $15,000 in cash boxes was stolen. Both gunmen jumped into a waiting car and sped away from their pursuers.

Three weeks later, two Italian immigrants were arrested for the crime. Nicola Sacco and Bartolomeo Vanzetti were not originally suspects, but at the time of their arrest, Sacco was carrying a gun and ammunition that was manufactured by the same company as the casings found at the scene. Further, they were active members of a radical anarchist group, and they both lied during questioning to protect their political comrades.

Anarchists believed in the overthrow of all central governments, by violence if necessary. Their history as political agitators in strikes and demonstrations severely damaged Sacco and Vanzetti's chances for a fair trial. They were found guilty of murder in the Boston courtroom of Judge Webster Thayer in 1921.

Six years of hearings and appeals followed. A murderer named Celestino Madeiros confessed to the Braintree payroll murders and said that the Joe Morelli gang participated with him.

The Sacco and Vanzetti case became a rallying cry for those opposed to the death penalty, including future Supreme Court Justice Felix Frankfurter, then a Harvard law professor. Millions saw it as a miscarriage of social justice. The governor of Massachusetts appointed a review committee, called the Lowell Committee because Harvard's president Abbott Lowell was head of the committee, but the committee supported the original verdict.

Protesters around the world held vigils for them, but Sacco and Vanzetti were executed in the electric chair on August 23, 1927.

> ## VIOLENCE OF THE STATE
>
> "The death penalty is a violent response to violence ... A state-sanctioned death penalty, rooted in ancient codes of revenge and retaliation, is more methodical and violent in its cold and unfeeling brutality than most crimes."
>
> —Billy Wayne Sinclair and Jodie Sinclair, authors of *Capital Punishment: An Indictment by a Death-Row Survivor*

Billy Wayne Sinclair and Jodie Sinclair, *Capital Punishment: An Indictment by a Death-Row Survivor.* New York, NY: Arcade Publishing, 2009, p. 26.

The Soviet Union was an ally of the United States during World War II, but following the war, Senator Joseph McCarthy and others whipped up paranoid fears of Soviet spies in every corner of the United States government. In an atmosphere of hysterical anticommunism, Governor Allan Shivers of Texas even suggested that mere membership in the Communist Party should be punishable by death.

During the Cold War, a period of ongoing political tension between the United States and the Soviet Union that lasted from 1947 to 1991, a handful of spies were prosecuted and executed for passing secrets to the Soviets. Most did not receive the death penalty but served some time in jail.

Support for the death penalty in the United States and in countries around the world declined throughout the late 20th century. Most countries outlawed the death penalty in the final decades of the 20th century, and as of 2017, 104 countries have abolished it for all crimes. Few countries now have public executions; more humane methods are used in most executions, but there are some notable exceptions. According to a 2017 report by the Transitional Justice Working Group (TJWG), "criminals" were publicly executed in common areas of North Korea to create fear throughout the dictatorship. These people were killed for things such as stealing rice and distributing or watching South Korean media. In Saudi Arabia, some offenders are still beheaded, and Iran still practices stoning to death. The Amnesty International organization stated that these executions were horrific and called on the Iranian government to stop the practice. In 2016, human rights activist and Iranian writer Golrokh Ebrahimi Iraee wrote an unpublished short story about stoning and received a six-year prison sentence. Amnesty International spoke out against this, calling her charges ludicrous and that she was "facing years behind bars simply for writing a story, and one which was not even published—she is effectively being punished for using her imagination."[7] In January 2017, she was released on bail.

The movement to abolish executions has been aided by Hollywood movies such as *Cell 2455 Death Row* (1955) and *Kill Me If You Can* (1977), which were based on the real-life story of Caryl Chessman; *In Cold Blood* (1967), which was based on the Truman Capote book of the same name and real-life 1959 murders of the Clutter family; *Dead Man Walking* (1995), which was based on the real-life murderer Robert Lee Willie; and *Monster* (2003), which was based on the serial killer Aileen Wuornos. Organizations and attorneys also mounted a series of legal challenges in the courts. From 1973 to 2017, 159 prisoners on death row have been exonerated, including 20 whose cases were cleared based on DNA evidence.

Kirk Bloodsworth's case is one of those cases. In 1985, Bloodsworth was handed a death penalty sentence for the rape and murder of a nine-year-old girl. Two young boys witnessed the girl walk into the forest with a man, whom they later described for authorities. Bloodsworth very slightly resembled this description, and despite witnesses placing him at home at the time of the murder and no physical evidence linking him to the murder, he was arrested and convicted. Throughout the nine years of his imprisonment, he wrote to numerous authorities and fought for his freedom because he did not commit the crime. Finally, Robert E. Morin, a lawyer at that time, was pushed by others to see Bloodsworth about a possible appeal. During his time in prison, Bloodsworth had read everything he could in the library and mentioned DNA testing to Morin. Morin did not think that there would be any DNA in the evidence to test; however, he was proved wrong. The DNA was analyzed and cleared

Bloodsworth, making him the first death row inmate to be exonerated based on DNA evidence. More than 20 years after being released from prison, he still has nightmares of being led to the death chamber and struggles every day with losing so much time due to a wrongful conviction—he was just 24 years old when he was given a death penalty sentence. Kirk Bloodsworth currently speaks publicly about his story and is an activist for death penalty abolition.

In the United States, many citizens continue to support capital punishment, even as opposition to it builds strength. A Pew Research Center poll in 2016 showed that 49 percent of Americans favor the death penalty, dropping 7 percent from a 2015 poll. This is more than 30 percent lower than the peak of support in 1994, when 80 percent of people supported the death penalty. When asked whether the death penalty was applied fairly, 44 percent of Americans said no.

Executions in the United States declined from the 1930s to the 1960s; in 1935, there were 199 executions, whereas from 1960 to 1976, there were a total of 191. Since 1976, 1,460 prisoners have been executed. Of the executions carried out in the last few years, 90 percent have come from 5 states: Texas, Oklahoma, Florida, Missouri, and Georgia. The 2008 Supreme Court case *Baze v. Rees* called into question the legality of lethal injection as a cruel and unusual punishment in violation of the Eighth Amendment to the U.S. Constitution. Some believed the Court's decision would reshape the states' use of capital punishment, but the Court ruled to permit lethal injection executions.

Support for the Death Penalty

Death penalty proponents have cited reasons such as retribution and deterrence as justification for keeping the death penalty. Supporters believe that capital punishment is justice for victims, stops other criminals from committing murder, and is preferred by the majority of citizens. Current polls, however, show that many of these reasons lack proof or support.

Evil Given for Evil Done

This justification for capital punishment is one of principle and dates back to the earliest philosophies of justice: Certain horrible crimes should be punished with equal violence in order to uphold the values of society. This reasoning suggests the death penalty is a moral necessity. The concept of retribution extends beyond the need for justice for victims' families; in fact, it channels what might be destructive acts of personal revenge into a controlled way to deal with anger and loss.

The counterargument to retribution as a moral imperative that enforces respect

Deterrance of future crimes is often cited as one reason for supporting capital punishment.

27

for the sanctity of life is the claim that capital punishment brutalizes society—that committing murder to avenge murder leads to less respect for life, not more. This side of the debate says that if the government represents all the members of society, then every member of society is individually responsible and accountable when someone is executed. This is an argument that dates back to Beccaria's 18th-century writings in *On Crimes and Punishments*.

> ## THE WORLD WOULD BE BLIND
>
> "We can argue all we like, but if capital punishment is being inflicted on some man, we are inclined to say: 'It serves him right.' That is not the spirit, I believe, in which legislation is enacted. If in this present age we were to go back to the old time of 'an eye for an eye and a tooth for a tooth,' there would be very few Honourable Gentlemen in this House who would not, metaphorically speaking, be blind and toothless."
>
> —George Perry Graham, a Canadian House of Parliament member debating capital punishment in 1914

Quoted in Ronald W. Nikkel, "The Heart of Justice," Prison Fellowship, October 31, 2011. www.prison-fellowship.org/2011/10/the-heart-of-justice/

Majority Rules

A majority of Americans still support capital punishment, although this support is at its lowest level since 1976. Capital punishment laws have been passed by 32 elected state legislatures. Death penalty advocates say these laws should not be nullified by a Supreme Court decision. In a democracy, the will of the people must count.

Opponents answer this argument by citing eras in American history such as the Cold War when the majority's fears instead of thoughtful analysis shaped public policy. Majorities in American history have made choices that, in hindsight, seem wrong. The District of Columbia and 18 states have abolished the death penalty.

Punishing Evil

Adolf Eichmann served with Hitler's Schutzstaffel (SS) forces at the Dachau Concentration Camp and then rose quickly in the ranks to become the director of the Reich Security Main Office's Jewish Affairs section, directly responsible for the deportation of more than 1.5 million Jews to death camps. After the defeat of the Nazi regime, he escaped from an American prison camp and hid in Argentina for 14 years until Israeli agents captured him and brought him to trial in Jerusalem. Eichmann's trial reminded people of the horrors of the Holocaust and society's responsibility to punish those who commit terrible acts. He was executed on May 31, 1962.

Moshe Landau, the presiding judge who sentenced Eichmann, said,

After considering the appropriate sentence for the Accused with a deep feeling of the burden of responsibility borne by us, we reached the conclusion that in order to punish the Accused and deter others, the maximum penalty laid down in the law must be imposed on him. In the Judgment we described the crimes in which the Accused took part. They are of unparalleled horror in their nature and their scope.[1]

Adolf Eichmann is shown here at his trial for mass murder.

1. Quoted in "The Trial of Adolf Eichmann, Session 121," The Nizkor Project, accessed September 15, 2017. www.nizkor.org/hweb/people/e/eichmann-adolf/transcripts/Sessions/Session-121-01.html.

> ### THE PUNISHMENT FITS THE CRIMES
>
> "Historically, the Eighth Amendment was understood to bar only those punishments that added 'terror, pain, or disgrace' to an otherwise permissible capital sentence ... I would not presume to tell parents whose life has been forever altered by the brutal murder of a child that life imprisonment is punishment enough."
>
> —Antonin Scalia, former associate justice of the U.S. Supreme Court

Quoted in "Top 10 Pro & Con Arguments," ProCon.org, updated December 9, 2016.

Scared Straight

The most common argument in favor of capital punishment is that it stops possible criminals because they fear their own death if they are caught. Studies of murder rates from states which have the death penalty and use it, those that have it on the books but do not execute killers, and states which have abolished capital punishment have led to confusing conclusions.

Some recent studies show that fear of the death penalty deters criminals. One study in 2006 by economists Hashem Dezhbakhsh and Joanna M. Shepherd examined each of the 50 states individually from 1960 to 2000; they reported that "capital punishment has a deterrent effect, and that executions have a distinct effect which [intensifies] the deterrent effect of merely (re)instating the death penalty."[8] The state of Illinois suspended executions starting in 2000, and just before he left office in 2003, Governor George Ryan commuted all the death row inmates' sentences to life imprisonment. In 2011, Illinois abolished the death penalty. Researchers Dale O. Cloninger and Roberto Marchesini examined the 4 years in Illinois without capital punishment and found "that approximately 150 additional homicides occurred in Illinois in the 48-month post-event period."[9]

Some researchers question the methods and samplings used in studies that support deterrence. These researchers point to other reports that show murder rates are unconnected to whether a state has or uses the death penalty. A 2012 review of current deterrence studies, conducted by the National Research Council, found that "research to date is not informative about whether capital punishment decreases, increases, or has no effect on homicide rates."[10]

Other researchers have found that the fear of being caught is more of a deterrent than capital punishment. Daniel S. Nagin found that "the evidence in support of the deterrent effect of the certainty of punishment is far more consistent than that for the severity of punishment."[11]

Critics also claim that murder is committed by people who cannot weigh consequences as others are able to, so the possibility of their own executions would not change their actions. However, capital crimes such as treason and assassination are planned by those who do calculate the consequences and who might be deterred by the death penalty. That possibility was a factor in the sentencing of Julius and Ethel Rosenberg, who were convicted of espionage (spying) in 1951.

Treason and the Death Penalty

The Cold War between the Soviet Union and the United States followed World War II. When the Soviets developed their own nuclear weapons just four years after the United States used atomic bombs at Hiroshima and Nagasaki, the belief was widespread that traitorous scientists in the United States must have leaked secrets to the Russians.

Julius Rosenberg was indeed such an informant. Rosenberg passed hundreds of technical reports to Soviet agents, and some evidence indicated that he recruited other spies who were sympathetic to the Communist cause. Ethel Rosenberg knew of her husband's work and helped the KGB (a Soviet security agency) recruit members.

The Rosenbergs' trial began on March 6, 1951, and they were soon convicted under the Espionage Act. Julius and Ethel Rosenberg were sent to the electric chair at Sing Sing Prison in New York on June 19, 1953. They were the only two American civilians to be executed for espionage during the Cold War. It was clear that in the fearful and accusatory atmosphere of the Cold War, a prime motive for their sentences was deterrence, especially in Ethel Rosenberg's case. Authors Ronald Radosh and Joyce Milton stated, "There was the very real desire to frighten other individuals who might potentially lend themselves to such activities in the future."[12]

Ethel and Julius Rosenberg, shown here, were executed after being found guilty for conspiracy to commit espionage.

Many who favor the death penalty recognize that conclusions on deterrence differ. They feel that until more definitive evidence is found, it is better to continue executing criminals. As John McAdams, political scientist at Marquette University, explained, "If we execute murderers and there is in fact no deterrent effect, we have killed a bunch of murderers. If we fail to execute murderers, and doing so would in fact have deterred other murders, we have allowed the killing of a bunch of innocent victims. I would much rather risk the former. This, to me, is not a tough call."[13]

Opponents collect studies that show no deterrence value to capital punishment. Canada, for instance, has not executed anyone since 1962 but has not experienced any increase in capital crime rates.

According to the American Civil Liberties Union (ACLU), "The vast preponderance of the evidence shows that the death penalty is no more effective than imprisonment in deterring murder and that it may even be an incitement to criminal violence. Death-penalty states as a group do not have lower rates of criminal homicide than non-death-penalty states."[14]

Protecting Society

Some criminals will never be rehabilitated. If they are imprisoned for life, they may become eligible for parole and commit additional murders. Some prisoners serving time for murder were previously convicted of another murder; if those prisoners had been executed the first time, lives would have been saved. Criminals that lead deadly gangs from inside prisons can still order the murder of people on the outside. Some people argue that protection of these new victims should be more important than the rights of convicted killers.

Another argument is that imprisoning murderers puts other prison inmates and guards at risk. Death penalty advocates believe that some killers must be executed to save others in their presence. Even lifetime imprisonment might not be a safe choice for some convicts, such as Jack Henry Abbott.

The Murderer and Norman Mailer

Jack Henry Abbott's early life was difficult: He grew up in foster care, juvenile detention homes, and reform school. At 21, he was serving a sentence for forgery in a Utah prison when he stabbed another inmate to death. He was given an additional

3 to 23 years for the murder and then escaped to Colorado, where he was apprehended in a bank robbery.

Saved Just in Time

John Smith, English burglar, 1705: John Smith was hanged at Tyburn gallows on December 12, 1705. He had been hanging for 15 minutes when a runner arrived, and as the crowd shouted for a reprieve, he was cut down and revived. Even though the reprieve turned out to be an elaborately staged hoax, he was legitimately pardoned and became a celebrity speaker. The story of "Half-Hanged Smith" comes from the Newgate Calendar, a sensationalist publication describing the crimes, trials, and executions of common criminals from Newgate Prison in London, England, intended as a moral lesson to the population.

Fyodor Dostoyevsky, Russian novelist, 1849: Dostoyevsky and his friends were sentenced to death by firing squad for subversive political activities. On the morning of December 22, 1849, as their hands were being bound for execution, a reprieve arrived from Czar Nicholas I. Instead of being shot, the men were to be deported to Siberia, where they would serve four years in a labor camp. Dostoyevsky went on to write novels, such as *Crime and Punishment* and *The Brothers Karamazov*, that some consider the greatest in literary history.

Russian prisoner, 1880s: Czar Alexander III wrote the death sentence of a prisoner in his own handwriting: "Pardon impossible, to be sent to Siberia." His wife believed the prisoner was innocent. She saved his life by moving the comma in the message so that it read, "Pardon, impossible to be sent to Siberia."[1]

1. Quoted in Emily Finch and Stefan Fafinski, *Criminology Skills*. Oxford, UK: Oxford University Press, 2012, p. 138.

Abbott read about *The Executioner's Song*, Norman Mailer's book about death row murderer Gary Gilmore, and began a long correspondence with Mailer. His brilliantly written letters about prison life were published by Mailer as *In the Belly of the Beast*, and several celebrities supported Abbott's parole in 1981. However, prison officials at the parole hearing testified to their fear that the killer was still a dangerous psychotic. Nonetheless, Abbott was released.

Just six weeks after he was released from prison, Abbott got into a trivial argument in a Manhattan restaurant and stabbed a man to death once again. He escaped but was apprehended several months later. In 2002, he hanged himself in his cell, but he never repented for the murders he committed.

Murder in the Commission of Another Crime

Many death row criminals have committed "felony murders," that is, killings that occurred during the commission of another crime, such as rape or burglary. If a victim dies in the course of a felony, whether or not the killer intended that death to occur, the defendant is guilty of first-degree murder and may be sentenced to death. For example, if an arsonist burns down a building and someone sleeping inside the building dies, the arsonist can be convicted of first-degree murder.

The argument is made that felons would kill even more victims as they committed crimes if there were no felony murder executions. With capital punishment hanging over their heads, criminals will not risk an escalation into violence; especially, they will not shoot the police who arrest them. The opposition viewpoint to this claim is that few criminals contemplate the consequences of getting caught.

Taxpayer Expenses for Punishment

The expense of keeping a prisoner alive for the rest of their life is often considered a powerful argument for execution over imprisonment without parole. Some people believe it is a waste of taxpayers' money to take care of society's worst citizens during a life imprisonment; they think this money could be better directed toward preventing crime through police work or education.

American tax dollars pay for a prisoner's sentence, whether it is life imprisonment or an execution.

However, dozens of state reports show that it actually costs more to execute a prisoner than it does to keep them alive for 40 or more years. Several studies have found that it costs nearly twice as much per inmate to maintain death row each day, as opposed to the cost of maintaining the average prisoner. In Oklahoma, the average case-level cost of the death penalty was $700,000 higher than life without parole cases. In California, the Commission on the Fair Administration of Justice found that the death penalty cost the state $137 million in 2008, versus an estimated $11.5 million per year for life in prison.

Capital punishment is so expensive because death row facilities, with their increased security and requirements for isolation from other prisoners, cost more than other prisons. However, the courtroom legal costs for repeated appeals of the sentence account for the majority of the expense. Advocates of the death penalty find the cost arguments in favor of life imprisonment unacceptable. They point out that if the death penalty opponents did not file so many appeals, the cost of execution would go down. Advocates also argue that the cost is less important than the state's ability to provide justice.

Rights of the Accused

In the United States, very few convicted murderers are sentenced to die—less than 2 percent. Death penalty advocates point to the many processes in place that protect the rights of the defendant in capital cases and work to reduce or reverse death sentences. If any procedural errors from the original trial can be substantiated on appeal, the accused receives a new trial.

The cost of housing a prisoner for the rest of their life versus executing the prisoner is often brought up in death penalty debates.

Harris County, Texas, home to the city of Houston, invokes the death penalty more frequently than any other county in the United States. According to the Texas Coalition to Abolish the Death Penalty, as of 2017, Harris County has executed 127 people, which is more than any other state except Texas—Texas has executed more than 540 people since 1982. In Texas, a jury does not focus on life versus death. Instead, their deliberations must answer three questions: "Is the defendant likely to be a future danger to society? If the defendant wasn't the actual killer, did he or she intend to kill someone or anticipate death? And, if the answer is yes to the previous questions, is there any mitigating evidence—like an intellectual disability—that the jury thinks warrants the lesser sentence of life without parole?"[15] To issue the death penalty, all 12 jurors must unanimously answer "no" to the last question and "yes" to the first two questions. The instructions state that 10 or more jurors must agree if they answer "yes" to the last question and "no" to the first two questions. However, what the jury instructions do not state is if just one juror disagrees with the rest on any of the questions, the sentence becomes life without parole.

JUSTICE FOR VICTIMS

"If a man steals your bicycle and society allows him to keep and ride around on that bicycle, most of us would find that profoundly unjust. Why, then, is it just to allow everyone who steals a life to keep his own?"

—Dennis Prager, columnist and radio talk show host

Dennis Prager, "There's a Moral Reason That McVeigh Must Die....," *Los Angeles Times*, June 8, 2001. articles.latimes.com/2001/jun/08/local/me-7840.

To pass a death penalty sentence, a grand jury must indict the accused on murder charges; a panel of judges must determine that the death penalty is possible in the case; attorneys must be assigned to the defendant whether or not they can afford them; money is awarded for the costs of investigating the case; the burden of proof beyond a reasonable doubt is on the prosecution; and the jury must unanimously agree on the death penalty. A separate sentencing phase begins once a guilty verdict is chosen. Mitigating circumstances are presented at that time; these are conditions of the case and the defendant, such as

Arguments for Capital Punishment

The death penalty is warranted, according to its supporters, for the following reasons:

1. *Retribution*: To take a moral stance against evil acts, society must punish its worst offenders with death and provide justice for victims.
2. *Deterrence*: Although studies seem contradictory, some believe that use of capital punishment deters criminals from committing murders.
3. *Protection of society from repeat killers*: If they had been executed the first time, the other victims of repeat murderers would never have died.
4. *Reduction of violence during other felonies*: Fear of the death penalty stops felons from committing other murders.
5. *Cost*: The money used to jail murderers for life is better spent on protection and education.
6. *Defendants' rights and rarity of executions*: Safeguards of killers' rights and elaborate appeal procedures lead to the execution of only a tiny fraction of murderers.
7. *Reprieves*: Even when all other procedures have not stopped an execution, clemency by the governor, the president, or the Supreme Court is possible.

poverty, child abuse, emotional or mental problems, or lack of a prior record, which can lessen the punishment. Whatever the sentence, the accused receives an automatic first appeal.

These procedures are standard across the United States. Opponents of capital punishment respond by citing inmates on death row whose innocence has been established by new DNA or other evidence, but who were convicted despite these safeguards.

Saved by the State: Reprieves

At the final hour, governors may grant a reprieve for a convict about to be executed. Proponents of the death penalty cite the commuted sentences of death row inmates as a final protection against unwarranted executions. In many states, review boards examine each case and recommend to the governor which prisoners should be offered clemency (reprieve).

Texas prisoner Kenneth Foster was just six hours away from a lethal injection when the sitting governor, Rick Perry, took the recommendation of the Texas Board of Pardons and Paroles, which had voted six to one to commute Foster's sentence to life imprisonment. Foster was the getaway driver in a 1996 robbery. His partner shot the victim as Foster sat 90 feet (27.4 m) away. Texas has a "Law of Parties" that considers those who had a major role in a capital crime as guilty as the actual killer. Newspapers around the state ran editorials calling for Foster's reprieve, citing too many Texas executions: 21 in the first half of 2007, and 400 in the state since the reinstatement of the death penalty in 1982.

In Connecticut, Georgia, and Idaho, a review board by itself may grant a reprieve, and in Nebraska, Nevada, and Utah, the governor sits on the board that decides upon clemency. The Supreme Court and the president of the United States can also grant reprieves. In the 1974 case of *Schick v. Reed*, the Supreme Court upheld the right of the president to grant not only a reprieve but the conditions that would accompany it—in the Schick case, life imprisonment without parole.

The Case Against the Death Penalty

Those against the death penalty have their own set of reasons and data. Arguments for abolishment focus on the effects of capital punishment and its fair use across all of society. As with claims supporting the death penalty, each argument attacking it also elicits opposing responses.

Inciting Violence

Some opponents go so far as to call the effect of executions "barbarous." Public violence, they say, encourages the disturbed citizens of society to commit more violence. For example, in the aftermath of the assassination of President John F. Kennedy, homicide rates rose. Terrorists and mass killers such as Dylann Roof, who was sentenced to death in 2017 for the 2015 murder of nine people at the Emanuel African Methodist Episcopal Church in Charleston, South Carolina, may actually be encouraged by the prospect of public execution; they desire the additional publicity for their causes that comes when they are executed. They may also seek self-importance as martyrs to those causes.

Beccaria wrote in 1764 that the death penalty reduces the sensitivity of society to human suffering. Opponents believe that even if deaths were physically painless (and many examples of electrocutions and hangings gone awry can be found), institutionalized murder causes psychological trauma to everyone in society.

According to the ACLU,

> A society that respects life does not deliberately kill human beings. An execution is a violent public spectacle of official homicide, and one that endorses killing to solve social problems—the worst possible

example to set for the citizenry, and especially children. Governments worldwide have often attempted to justify their lethal fury by extolling the purported benefits that such killing would bring to the rest of society. The benefits of capital punishment are illusory, but the bloodshed and the resulting destruction of community decency are real.[16]

Death penalty advocates deny the brutalization argument by pointing to countries with higher execution rates than the United States:

A crime is an unlawful act, legal punishment is a lawful act ... There is no evidence for brutalization caused by the death penalty. The idea that legal killing will lead to imitation by illegal killing, or to any increase in violent crime, is unsubstantiated. And proponents do not explain why legal imprisonment does not lead to kidnappings, or why violent crime in Singapore and Saudi Arabia, both renowned for executions and physical punishments, is so infrequent.[17]

Americans are almost evenly divided on whether the death penalty is morally wrong or a necessary part of the justice system.

Opponents say the cost to morality is unbearably high if executions do not save innocent future victims, while supporters justify violence to evildoers because their studies show that the death penalty is a deterrent to possible killers.

Wrongful Death: Executing the Innocent

According to the Death Penalty Information Center's Innocence List, 159 death row inmates have been exonerated since 1973. To be included on the Innocence List, defendants must have been convicted and sentenced to death, and their convictions must then have been overturned. Some were acquitted when they were retried, or all charges were dropped against them, or they were given an absolute pardon by the governor after new evidence was uncovered. The average sentence a convict served before they were exonerated and released from prison was nine and a half years.

How do these innocent people end up on death row? The Death Penalty Information Center cites these common causes: "official misconduct," "perjury or false accusation," "false or misleading forensic evidence," "inadequate legal defense," "false or fabricated confession," and "mistaken eyewitness identification."[18] DNA analysis has been used by forensic scientists to free 20 of the 159 exonerated prisoners.

Those numbers are significant to death penalty opponents. Even more frightening are the numbers who were not saved before their executions. According to *Huffington Post*, "At least 39 executions are claimed to have been carried out in the U.S. in the face of evidence of innocence or serious doubt about guilt."[19]

The Cost of False Identification

In the 1980s, 17-year-old Ruben Cantu and 15-year-old David Garza were accused of breaking into an unfinished house in San Antonio, Texas, and shooting two construction workers with a rifle. One of the laborers, Juan Moreno, survived. Three times, Moreno refused to identify the picture of Cantu as one of his attackers.

Months later, Cantu shot and injured an off-duty policeman who provoked him in a bar incident, and Moreno was brought in again and pressured to identify Cantu for the murder at the construction site. This time, Moreno identified the defendant, but he later admitted to falsely identifying Cantu and said that the man who shot the rifle looked nothing like Cantu.

Without physical evidence, Cantu was convicted solely on the basis of Moreno's later recanted testimony. On August 24, 1993, Cantu was executed by lethal injection.

Garza, who has confessed since to involvement in the burglary and murder, has asserted that his accomplice was not Cantu. He indicated that Cantu was not present the night of the murder.

In recent years, some cases have been reviewed after the execution of an inmate and evidence of their wrongful conviction has been assured. One such case was of Cameron Todd Willingham. Willingham was convicted in 1992 of starting a house fire that killed his three daughters. He was executed in 2004. Afterward, forensic examiners found that the evidence used was incorrect. According to chemist Gerald Hurst, "There's nothing to suggest to any reasonable arson investigator that this was an arson fire. It was just a fire."[20] The Innocence Project later sued the state of Texas on behalf of the family to clear Willingham's name posthumously (after his death).

> **EFFECTS ON JURORS**
>
> "Did anybody know about this prior to his execution? Now I will have to live with this for the rest of my life. Maybe this man was innocent."
>
> —Juror Dorinda Brokofsky, commenting on the change of evidence in the case against Cameron Todd Willingham
>
> Quoted in Steve Mills and Maurice Possley, "Man Executed on Disproved Forensics," *Chicago Tribune*, December 9, 2004. www.chicagotribune.com/news/nationworld/chi-041209069dec09-story.html.

Is the Death Penalty Randomly Applied?

Opponents of capital punishment denounce the unpredictable choices of judges and juries. They say that sometimes criminals who commit the most terrible acts can be appealing in the courtroom and thus receive imprisonment, while people who commit lesser crimes but are not sympathetic receive the death penalty. Statistics show that women are rarely sentenced to death, while African Americans in southern states are overrepresented on death row. Geography, politics, and the quality of a defendant's lawyer also play unfair roles in punishments.

In the case of *Furman v. Georgia* (1972), the Supreme Court recognized a lack of uniformity in how death penalty defendants were sentenced. Justice Potter Stewart wrote for the majority that a random handful of defendants had been singled out for death, and it seemed that race played a part in the selection.

The dissenting justices in the Furman case argued that capital punishment had always been considered an appropriate punishment in the American legal tradition, and that the Constitution recognizes the death penalty in the 14th Amendment, which refers to the taking of life ("Nor shall any State deprive any person of life, liberty, or property, without due process of law").

The Furman case suspended capital punishment for four years while states acted to correct the inconsistencies of sentencing. Many states ordered that capital cases be tried in two parts, the first to determine guilt and the second to impose punishment. Standards were written to guide the discretion of judges and juries. When the death penalty was brought before the Supreme Court again in 1976 in *Gregg v. Georgia*, the Court decided that most states had fixed the inconsistency problem and could execute defendants; states that had responded with statutes that ordered the death penalty automatically upon conviction in certain felonies had these statutes struck down.

Since 1976, opponents have cited inconsistencies that continue. Some states, regions, and counties are overrepresented in death penalty statistics; for instance, Oklahoma and Tulsa counties in Oklahoma account for more than half of the death penalty convictions in the state, while five smaller counties make up a third of the number of convictions. Harris County in Texas, which incorporates Houston, is responsible for the most executions between 1976 and 2017, with Oklahoma County third. Between 2010 and 2014, Maricopa County in Arizona was the second highest producer of death penalty convictions, only slightly behind Los Angeles County in California, even though Los Angeles County has twice the population.

Courts continue to spare the death penalty for women. Even though women are arrested for 1 in 10 murders, they represent just 1 in 50 death sentences and only 1 in 100 executions.

Defendants on death row are frequently defended by incapable lawyers. A Dallas newspaper investigation in 2000 revealed that one in four death row inmates was defended by a lawyer who was eventually disciplined, suspended, or banned from practicing law by the state bar. Supreme Court Justice Ruth Bader Ginsburg said in 2001 that defendants with good lawyers do not get the death penalty; she added, "I have yet to see a death case among the dozens coming to the Supreme Court on eve-of-execution stay applications in which the defendant was well represented at trial."[21]

> ## CHANGING AMERICAN POLITICS
>
> "We will abolish the death penalty, which has proven to be a cruel and unusual form of punishment. It has no place in the United States of America. The application of the death penalty is arbitrary and unjust. The cost to taxpayers far exceeds those of life imprisonment. It does not deter crime. And, exonerations show a dangerous lack of reliability for what is an irreversible punishment."
>
> —Democratic Platform Committee, presented at the Democratic National Convention in 2016

"2016 Democratic Party Platform," The American Presidency Project, July 21, 2016, p 16.

Juveniles and the Death Penalty

Death penalty opponents are particularly upset by the execution of minors. They believe that young people are not as responsible for their acts as adults are and that they may be rehabilitated as they grow into adulthood. Therefore, executions of young teenagers are often cited by opposition writers in their rationales.

In 1988, the Supreme Court case of *Thompson v. Oklahoma* held that execution of a prisoner who had committed a crime when they were 15 or younger was cruel and unusual punishment, prohibited by the Eighth Amendment to the Constitution. Before the Thompson case, some states had no threshold age for executions at all. However, at the time, this ruling only affected three death row inmates in the United States: Wayne Thompson, Paula Cooper, and Troy Dugar. All three committed murders when they were 15 years old, while the other death row inmates had been older when they committed their crimes.

In 1946, 14-year-old James Lewis Jr. and 14-year-old Charles Trudell, who worked in a sawmill in Natchez, Mississippi, robbed their boss and killed him during the course of the robbery. They confessed to the crime. In separate trials, they were each convicted and sentenced to death. The press and radio were drawn to the case because the boys were so young, and support poured in from around the country to stop the executions.

Troy Dugar, shown here, received a death sentence that was changed after a Supreme Court ruling.

An attorney for Lewis and Trudell wrote in his local newspaper:

It occurs to my mind that neither of the children is sufficiently large to fit into the various attachments of the electric chair. Therefore, I should like to respectfully suggest that we seat them as we do children at our dinner table, that we place books underneath them in order that their heads should be at the proper height to receive the death current; and I further urge that the books used for this purpose be the "Age of Reason," "The Rise of Democracy in America," a copy of the Constitution of the United States, and an appropriately bound edition of the Holy Bible. Then, with one current of electricity, the state of Mississippi can destroy all simultaneously.[22]

Despite national protests, electrocution instruments were adjusted to the children's measurements, and they were executed in 1947.

In *Stanford v. Kentucky* (1989), the Supreme Court held that the Eighth Amendment to the U.S. Constitution does not prohibit the death penalty for crimes committed at ages 16 or 17. The sentence of Kevin Stanford, who had just turned 17 when he committed the brutal rape and murder of a gas station attendant, was upheld.

In 2005, the Court heard the case of *Roper v. Simmons* and ruled in a close 5–4 decision that the execution of offenders who were under the age of 18 when their crimes were committed was unconstitutional. Christopher Simmons, an abused 17-year-old Missouri boy who took drugs, had planned and executed the murder of Shirley Crook, whom he bound and threw into a river. His defense attorneys did not present evidence of his troubled youth or his drug abuse, but the crime was clearly premeditated and heinous. His appeal made it all the way to the Supreme Court; Roper, named in the case, was the director of the Missouri prison where Simmons sat on death row.

Legal briefs were submitted by medical and psychological organizations attesting to the difference between a teenage brain and an adult one and to teenagers' incomplete faculties of reasoning and decision making. Dozens of Nobel Peace Prize winners also wrote a brief urging the end of the death penalty for offenders who were not considered old enough to vote, serve in the military, or, in many states, to marry.

Justice Antonin Scalia wrote a dissenting opinion to the decision. He attacked the idea that public opinion had created a national agreement against execution of juveniles, since 18 of the 38 states that had capital punishment on the books still allowed it for 16- and 17-year-olds. More important, Scalia argued that the important issue was not present-day consensus but rather whether execution of juveniles was considered cruel and unusual when the Bill of Rights was ratified.

He challenged the right of the Court to determine moral values and impose them on the people; this, he wrote, was the role of the elected legislature.

Execution of the Disabled

Opponents of the death penalty believe that the intellectually disabled and the mentally ill are not in control of their acts and therefore cannot be punished for them in the same way society punishes those who can think clearly and see the consequences of their choices. Especially in the case of intellectual disability, the Court has limited the use of the death penalty.

In 1989, the Supreme Court dealt with diminished mental capacity in sentencing in the case of *Penry v. Lynaugh*. Penry, who raped and stabbed a woman to death, had a mental age of six and a half, although he was chronologically twenty-two years old. His IQ was that of a mild to moderately intellectually disabled individual. The Court decided that execution of individuals with an intellectual disability was not in violation of the Eighth Amendment against cruel and unusual punishments; intellectual disability was instead just a mitigating factor to be considered by the judges and juries during sentencing.

The Court did strike down the execution of the intellectually disabled in 2002 in *Atkins v. Virginia*. Daryl Atkins had prior felony convictions; he and an accomplice had driven their victim to an ATM, and one of them shot the victim to death. Each of the defendants said the other had done the shooting, but the jury blamed Atkins. On appeal, the defense had Atkins evaluated by a psychologist, who found him to be mildly intellectually disabled. The majority opinion by Justice John Paul Stevens argued that the main purposes of capital punishment, retribution and deterrence, would not be served by executing intellectually disabled individuals. Such defendants could not be held accountable for their actions in the same way as people of average intelligence, Stevens wrote, and the death penalty had to be eliminated as punishment for them, although other consequences were appropriate.

A 2014 Supreme Court case, *Hall v. Florida*, determined that states had to look beyond intelligence quotient (IQ) tests to establish intellectual disability. The court agreed that other factors, such as social skills and the presence of intellectual challenges before the age of 18, were important in deciding if a defendant was disabled. The court also allowed for errors in IQ testing, saying that a defendant who scored between 70 and 75 (out of 161 for adults or 162 for minors) should be able to present clinical testimony to prove their disability.

Mental illness as a mitigating factor was decided in the Florida case of *Ford v. Wainwright* in 1986. Alvin Bernard Ford, convicted of murder and sent to death row in 1974, was clearly mentally ill; he referred to himself as the pope, said he had appointed nine new justices to the Florida Supreme Court, and

"I Am a Human Being"

David Lawson, age 38, was executed for murdering Wayne Shinn, who had caught Lawson breaking into his house in 1980.

Sister Helen Prejean is a famous death penalty opponent. Her story has been told in the press and in the award-winning film *Dead Man Walking*. Prejean wrote about Lawson's execution:

David Lawson chose to die in the gas chamber. He said he wanted the people of North Carolina to know they were killing a man ... In a last appeal to the U.S. Supreme Court, David Lawson's lawyers requested a stay of execution, arguing that execution by gas was a form of cruel punishment and in violation of the Eighth Amendment, but the Court refused to hear the petition ...

It took thirteen minutes for the gas to kill him ...

Soon after 2:00 a.m., the cyanide was dropped into the acid and the lethal fumes began to rise. Lawson, choking and gasping and straining against the straps, took short breaths and cried out, "I am human. I am a human being." ... Drool

The Case Against the Death Penalty

claimed he was free to leave the prison any time he wanted. A panel of psychiatrists examined him and decided that Ford was mentally ill but could still understand the nature of the death penalty. Ford sued Louie L. Wainwright, the director of the Florida Department of Corrections. The majority decision by Justice Thurgood Marshall asserted that the execution of the seriously mentally ill was morally wrong and did not serve any of the goals of capital punishment. The opinion also required adequate procedures for determining the mental competence of defendants.

Although intellectual disabilities are now taken into account more often, many of those on death row suffer from impaired thinking. A 2014 *Hastings Law Journal* review of the last 100 people executed found "that the overwhelming

and tears slid from under the mask. A few deep breaths of the gas would have killed him sooner, but David Lawson continued to take short breaths and despite paroxysms of choking cried out until his voice was but a whisper: "I ... am ... a ... human ... being."[1]

Sister Helen Prejean is shown here counseling a man on death row at the Louisiana State Penitentiary.

1. Helen Prejean, *The Death of Innocents: An Eyewitness Account of Wrongful Executions*. New York, NY: Random House, 2005, pp. 264–265.

majority of executed offenders suffered from intellectual impairments, were barely into adulthood, wrestled with severe mental illness, or endured profound childhood trauma. Most executed offenders fell into two or three of these core mitigation areas, all which are characterized by significant intellectual and psychological deficits."[23]

A PAINLESS PENALTY

"Americans tend to want the death penalty to be as sanitary as possible. It's an act of state violence, but we don't want it to be violent."

—Andrew Novak, George Mason University professor

Quoted in Amelia Thomson-DeVeaux, "Is The Firing Squad More Humane Than Lethal Injection?," FiveThirtyEight, March 2, 2017. fivethirtyeight.com/features/is-the-firing-squad-more-humane-than-lethal-injection/.

Race and Capital Punishment

Opponents of the death penalty have conducted statistical studies over many years that show the race of the defendant frequently determines whether the death penalty is applied. Studies of capital punishment show that more death sentences and executions occur in southern states than elsewhere in the United States and that black convicts are overrepresented on death row and in actual executions.

In 1944, Gunnar Myrdal published *An American Dilemma: The Negro Problem and Modern Democracy*. This study was funded by the Carnegie Foundation, which chose a non-American to conduct the research in order to remain unbiased. Myrdal found clear evidence that black Americans were executed much more often than people of other races who had committed similar crimes. He said this was due to a legacy of slavery, which prejudiced some southern juries against African Americans. Slaves had been considered dangerous and aggressive by their owners, who feared uprisings such as the one led by Nat Turner, in which the rebellion of 75 slaves resulted in the murder of more

Race of Defendants Executed in the U.S. Since 1976

race	percentage
Latino	8.3%
White	55.6%
Black	34.5%
Other	1.6%

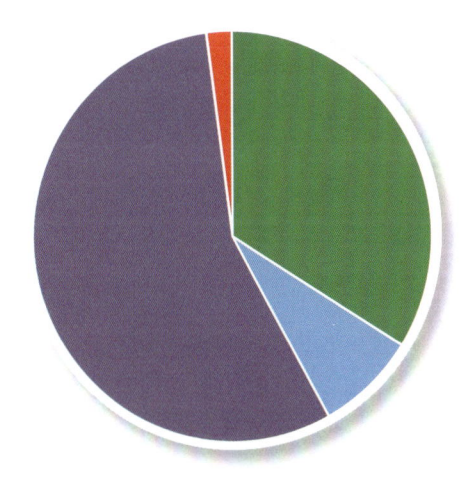

Race of Victims Since 1976

race	percentage
Latino	6.9%
White	75.6%
Black	15.3%
Other	2.1%

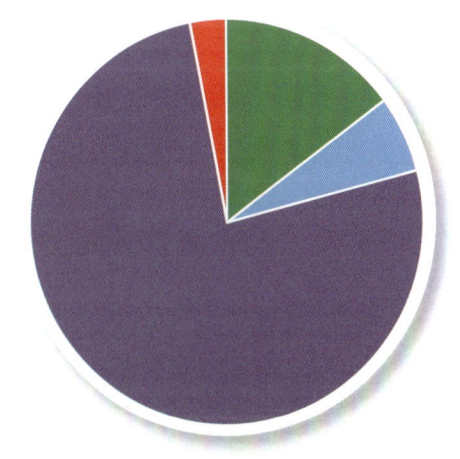

Current U.S. Death Row Population by Race

race	percentage
Latino	13.19%
White	42.38%
Black	41.65%
Other	2.78%

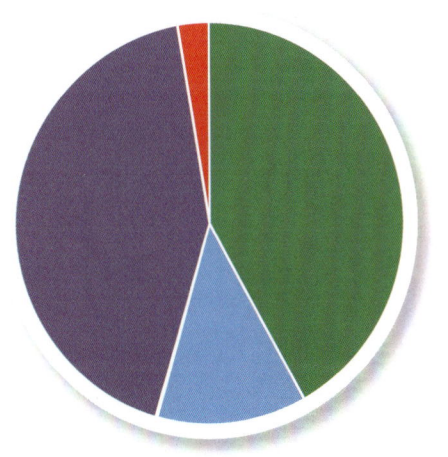

Race plays a role in who receives the death penalty, as this information from the National Association for the Advancement of Colored People's (NAACP) Legal Defense and Educational Fund (LDF) shows.

than 50 whites. This conception continued into the modern era to influence the minds of some people, particularly in the South. "Of the 3,334 people executed in this country between 1930 and 1967 for the crime of murder, 2,066 of them were black. Of the 435 executed for rape; 405 were black."[24] From 1976 to 2017, 1,460 prisoners were executed in the United States, and 34.5 percent of them were black.

Studies in individual states confirm that race and geography play a role in death sentences. Even in federal capital cases, this is true: In 2000, the Justice Department reported that in 80 percent of the 682 cases sent to the department for approval to seek the death penalty, the defendants were people of color. Additionally, 40 percent of the cases were filed in just 5 jurisdictions. Attorney General Janet Reno announced that she was troubled by these statistics and ordered investigations of the racial and ethnic disparities.

The race of the victim also prejudices death row outcomes. The killing of a white person brings the defendant a death sentence more often than the killing of a person of color. The Fair Punishment Project found, in looking at the top 16 death penalty counties, a persistent bias against defendants of color. Between 2010 and 2015, no white person was given the death penalty for killing a black person in 14 of the counties. The opposite was true for black defendants: They were more likely to be given the death penalty if their victim was white. In the 16 counties studied, 46 percent of death penalty recipients were black; 73 percent of those given the death penalty were people of color. Professors Jack Boger and Isaac Unah of the University of North Carolina analyzed the records of 502 murder trials in that state between 1993 and 1997 and found that the race of the victim prejudiced the sentencing outcomes. They found that defendants whose victims are white are three and a half times more likely to be sentenced to death than those whose victims were people of color. Unah said, "The odds are supposed to be zero that race plays a role. No matter how the data was analyzed, the race of the victim always emerged as an important factor in who received the death penalty."[25]

Jury selection slants outcomes as well, the opponents claim. A prosecutor in Alabama disqualified several jurors because they were affiliated with Alabama State University, a predominantly black campus. Dobie Gillis Williams, whose story was told by prominent death penalty opponent Sister Helen Prejean, was tried by an all-white jury; the black members of the jury panel were all struck from the jury by the prosecutor. Williams was executed in 1999. Bias against Latinx defendants was shown to be prominent in Southern California, based on a 2014 study of white and Latinx individuals called for jury duty. White jurors were more likely to give the death penalty to defendants who were Latinx and poor; Latinx jurors showed no such bias against white defendants.

Racial slurs in courtrooms may go unnoticed or unpunished. The Florida Supreme Court upheld the sentence of a defendant whose white judge used such language in open court. In Missouri, Judge Earl Blackwell, who is white, presided over a murder case in which the defendant, Brian Kinder, was an unemployed black man. Blackwell told the press he was changing political parties because he did not favor helping minorities: "The truth is that I have noticed in recent years that the Democrat party places far too much emphasis on representing minorities such as homosexuals, people who don't want to work, and people with a skin that's any color but white."[26] Kinder's lawyer made a motion to have the judge disqualify himself on the basis of prejudice, but it was denied.

Another case of racial prejudice came before the U.S. Supreme Court in 2017. In the case of *Buck v. Davis*, the defendant was sentenced to death for murdering his ex-girlfriend and a male friend. The state of Texas can only hand down the death penalty if the judge reasonably believes the defendant will go on to commit further violent acts. During his trial, a psychologist called by Buck's lawyer testified that if the defendant were released he would commit more crimes because he was black. After an appeal, the Texas courts originally upheld the death penalty, but the case continued on to the U.S. Supreme Court, which overturned the ruling because of racial bias. Chief Justice John Roberts said in the court's opinion, "When a jury hears expert testimony that expressly makes a defendant's race directly pertinent on the question of life or death, the impact of that evidence cannot be measured simply by how much air time it received at trial or how many pages it occupies in the record. Some toxins can be deadly in small doses."[27]

IS THE DEATH PENALTY MORAL?

"When I was elected I was pro-death penalty—an eye for an eye, a tooth for a tooth. I've come 180 degrees. It's not cost effective, it doesn't do any benefit, it really divides … there's no deterrence, whether you have the death penalty or not, the same amount of crime, the same amount of heinous violent murders. (It's) the ultimate moral question. My job is to call up some jailer down in Cañon City and tell him to kill somebody he doesn't want to kill. That's just morally a very difficult position."

—Colorado Governor John Hickenlooper Jr.

Quoted in Mike Littwin, "The Death Penalty Conversation in Colorado Just Grew a Lot Louder," *The Colorado Independent*, April 21, 2017. www.coloradoindependent.com/165006/littwin-death-penalty-hickenlooper-dunlap-gorsuch-lee.

Cruel and Unusual Punishment

Arguments that any form of execution constitutes cruel and unusual punishment stem from the Eighth Amendment to the Constitution, which reads, "Excessive bail shall not be required, nor excessive fines imposed, nor cruel and unusual punishments inflicted."

Opponents believe that execution is, in and of itself, cruel and unusual. They enumerate the horror stories of specific execution methods that cause slow and painful death. Supporters of the death penalty respond to the claims of cruel and unusual punishment by pointing out that the death row inmates' victims were human beings too. Most of the victims, they say, suffered much more painful deaths than those inflicted by lethal injection, the most common execution method in the United States today.

Arguments Against the Death Penalty

The death penalty is opposed for the following reasons:
1. *Brutalization*: The death penalty increases violence in society and turns society into accomplices to institutionalized murder.
2. *Execution of innocents*: Judges and juries have made mistakes, and the blood of innocent people is on everyone's hands.
3. *Inconsistency*: Some convicts are sentenced to die who have committed less horrible crimes than others whose lives are spared.
4. *Execution of juveniles*: Teenagers do not have adult judgment and control—mitigating factors that should spare their lives.
5. *Intellectual disability and mental illness*: Intellectual disabilities and mental illness must also be mitigating factors to spare defendants' lives.
6. *Racism*: Discrimination against minority defendants and in favor of white victims causes those defendants to be sentenced too often to death.
7. *Cruel and unusual punishment*: Execution is, in and of itself, cruel, and botched executions are a form of public torture.

Opponents of capital punishment give many reasons for their position.

Opponents say excessive wait times and state mismanagement can amount to torture for people on death row. Prisoners awaiting execution wait on average 25 years for their sentence to be carried out. In a 2015 California court case, *Jones v. Davis*, Judge Cormac J. Carney noted that of the 900 people sentenced to death since 1978, only 13 had been executed. Judge Carney ruled California's death penalty unconstitutional due to these delays and said most prisoners "will have languished for so long on death row that their execution will serve no retributive or deterrent purpose and will be arbitrary."[28]

Austin Sarat, a political science professor at Amherst College, released a book in 2014 called *Gruesome Spectacles: Botched Executions and America's Death Penalty*. Sarat found that in the 8,776 executions between 1890 and 2010, 276 were botched in some way. These included leaking gas chambers, incorrect use of lethal drugs, and electric chairs that caused burning or fires. These botched executions are seen by opponents of the death penalty as forms of public torture.

The Court's Rule on Capital Punishment

The Supreme Court of the United States has taken up cases for and against the death penalty. Since at least 1968, major court decisions have changed the way the United States implements death sentences. Each case presents a step forward as a society—the people are deciding whether capital punishment should exist in a civilized nation.

Many death penalty supporters feared—and opponents hoped—that the case of *Baze v. Rees*, which the Court decided in 2008, would provide a clear opening for the Court to rule that any executions by lethal injection (and perhaps, by eventual extension, other methods) was a cruel and unusual punishment and thus unconstitutional. However, the Court ruled in April 2008 that lethal injection executions do not violate the Eighth Amendment, and thus that they could continue throughout the United States. A second court decision in 2015, *Glossip v. Gross*, again ruled that lethal injection was not cruel and unusual.

A case can make its way to the Supreme Court in three different ways. The first is an appeal based on facts from the original trial; the second is based on new evidence or lawyer problems. These appeals have to make their way through various levels of lower courts before the Supreme Court will consider hearing them. The third type of appeal is based on a possible violation of the Constitution, which must go directly into the federal court system. When the Supreme Court makes a decision in a case, it dictates policy for all 50 states.

Witherspoon Starts the Death Penalty Debate

In 1968, William G. Witherspoon was convicted of shooting a policeman to death in Chicago, Illinois. Illinois law permitted the automatic exclusion of any juror in a potential death penalty case who was opposed to or had doubts against the death

On a number of occasions, the U.S. Supreme Court has ruled on cases related to the death penalty, including defining eligible crimes and acceptable execution methods.

penalty. Witherspoon appealed the state court's guilty verdict on the basis of the bias of the jury. He claimed that those who accepted capital punishment would be more likely to find him guilty than the population at large.

In the majority decision, Justice Potter Stewart wrote that the Court reversed Witherspoon's sentence because the systematic exclusion of jurors who were unsure about capital punishment deprived him of an impartial hearing. The only jurors who could be excluded were those who said they would automatically vote against the death penalty in all cases.

Witherspoon v. Illinois was the first case that showed that the Supreme Court was willing to limit state practices in capital cases, and it opened the door to 40 years of subsequent Supreme Court decisions on the death penalty.

Furman Cases Reverse the Death Penalty

In 1972, the National Association for the Advancement of Colored People's (NAACP) Legal Defense and Educational Fund (LDF) mounted a campaign to bring the entire issue of capital punishment to the Supreme Court as a violation of the 8th and 14th Amendments to the Constitution. Three cases were grouped together to be heard by the Court under the title of *Furman v. Georgia*.

The LDF argued that evolving decency standards made the death penalty unacceptable, even though 40 states had it on their books. The only reason this was so, the LDF said, was that the enforcement of it was so rare; only a handful of poor, minority convicts were ever put to death, and this was why the American public looked the other way. It was cruel and unusual punishment to single out this small group of people for a consequence

Ronald Reagan, shown here during his time as governor of California, was opposed to the abolition of the death penalty.

that would be condemned if it were doled out evenhandedly and more widely.

Lawyers for the states protested that the Court did not have the ability to make laws for the people, which only legislatures in the states could do. If the death penalty was applied in a biased way, the issue was equal protection under the 14th Amendment and not the legality of capital punishment altogether. Furthermore, the small fraction of executions showed not prejudice but extreme care by judges and juries.

The justices of the Supreme Court did not issue the usual majority and minority decisions: Each justice authored their own. The decision was 5–4 to abolish capital punishment as practiced in the Furman cases, because it was cruel and unusual punishment under the Eighth Amendment. Each of the dissenting justices wrote an opinion agreeing with the defense that the issue was one for state legislatures, not for the Court, which was invading the power of those legislatures.

At the same time as the verdict was announced, the Court reversed the death sentences in 100 capital cases under appeal. The decision suspended the capital punishment laws of the United States as they were written at the time and saved the lives of 63 inmates facing execution around the country.

THE CONSTITUTION AND THE DEATH PENALTY

"Capital punishment presents moral questions that philosophers, theologians, and statesmen have grappled with for millennia. The Framers of our Constitution disagreed bitterly on the matter. For that reason, they handled it the same way they handled many other controversial issues: they left it to the People to decide."

—Antonin Scalia, former associate justice of the U.S. Supreme Court

Quoted in Charlie Savage, "Highlights from the Supreme Court Decision on Lethal Injection," *New York Times*, June 8, 2015. www.nytimes.com/interactive/2015/us/2014-term-supreme-court-decision-lethal-injection.html?mcubz=3.

Conservatives around the country, led by President Richard Nixon, strongly opposed the Furman verdict. They worked to reinstate the death penalty by fixing inconsistencies in state sentencing laws and providing clearer guidelines for judges and juries to follow in capital cases.

> ### CONSIDER VICTIMS' PAIN FIRST
>
> "While there's always going to [be] a risk of some pain in an execution because it can be difficult to find veins, the 'incomparable suffering the victim endured during the last desperate minutes of her life' must not be ignored."
>
> —Alex Kozinski, former chief judge of the U.S. Court of Appeals for the Ninth Circuit

Quoted in Associated Press. "Federal Judges Consider Victims' Pain over That of Death Row Inmates," *Death Penalty News*, May 21, 2012. deathpenaltynews.blogspot.com/2012/05/federal-judges-consider-victims-pain.html.

Executions Resume

The case of *Gregg v. Georgia* in 1976 was the result of efforts to reform death penalty statutes in the states and reinstate capital punishment, and these efforts were successful. The Court ruled that the new death penalty statutes in Florida, Georgia, and Texas fulfilled the requirements set out in *Furman v. Georgia* for objectivity in sentencing. Inmates sentenced under such laws could be executed, wrote the majority. Executions resumed in 1977.

Challenging the Death Penalty

Furman v. Georgia had struck down the death penalty because of the wide latitude some states afforded in capital cases for juries and judges to send defendants to death row. North Carolina responded to this critique by removing the jurists' power altogether and prescribing the death penalty for every first-degree murder conviction. In the 1976 case of *Woodson v. North Carolina*, the Supreme Court found this equally unacceptable. The justices decided that North Carolina was not granting enough latitude to consider mitigating factors. The Court was carefully narrowing the use of the death penalty it had restored under *Gregg v. Georgia*.

Executions in the United States Since Furman Was Set Aside (1977 to 2016)

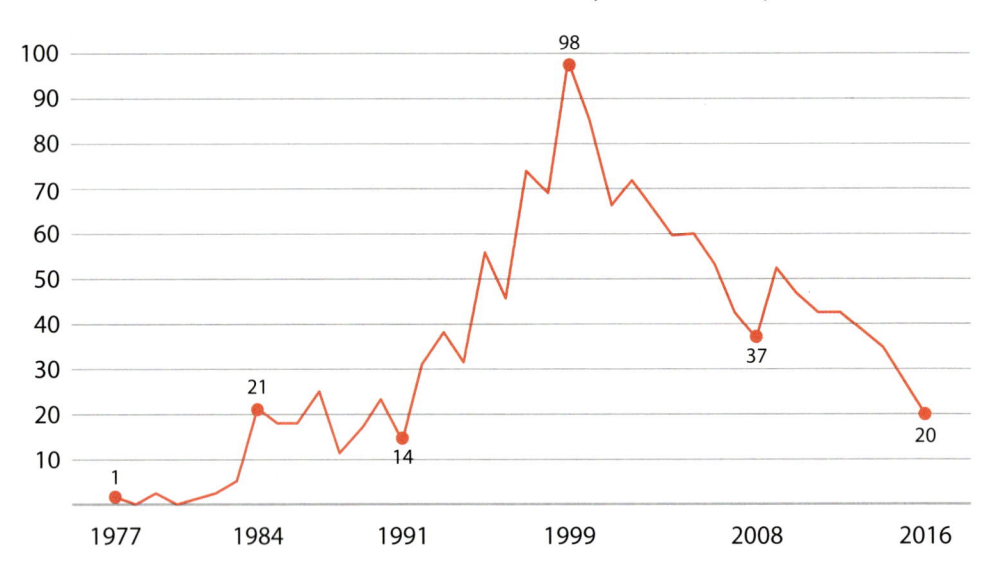

As this information from the Death Penalty Information Center shows, executions in the United States reached a high point in 1999.

Jury Bias

In 1987, the NAACP LDF brought the case of *McCleskey v. Kemp* to the Supreme Court. Warren McCleskey was a black man convicted of killing a white Atlanta, Georgia, police officer and sentenced to death in the electric chair by 11 white jurors and only 1 black juror. The LDF based its case on a study of Georgia death penalty cases by David Baldus, a professor at the University of Iowa. The Baldus study analyzed 2,000 murder cases in Georgia and showed that black defendants received the death penalty more often than white defendants; the difference was even more striking when comparing death penalty sentences for black defendants who killed white victims to sentences for white defendants who killed black victims.

In the opinion of the Court in the case of *McCleskey v. Kemp*, Justice Lewis Powell reviewed the study:

> *The Baldus study is actually two sophisticated statistical studies that examine over 2,000 murder cases that occurred in Georgia during the 1970's. The raw numbers collected by Professor Baldus indicate that defendants charged with killing white persons received the death penalty in 11% of the cases, but defendants charged with killing blacks received the death penalty in only 1% of the cases. The raw numbers also indicate a reverse racial disparity according to the race of the defendant: 4% of the black defendants received the death penalty, as opposed to 7% of the white defendants.*[29]

The LDF claimed that capital punishment was not doled out with an even hand in Georgia, violating the 14th Amendment's guarantee of equal protection of the laws. An outcome for the defense could overturn capital punishment altogether, as tainted by racism.

The Supreme Court's 5–4 majority decision against McCleskey was written by Justice Powell, who found that in McCleskey's individual case, no specific bias of the jury had been shown, even though the general difference between the treatment of black and white defendants was established in the Baldus report. The decision was considered a major victory for death penalty proponents and a serious blow to death penalty abolitionists.

Execution of a Juvenile: The Thompson Case

William Wayne Thompson, a 15-year-old boy, participated in his brother-in-law's murder in Oklahoma. He could be tried as an adult under Oklahoma law if the court decided that the crime justified it. He was convicted as an adult and sentenced to death. In the *Thompson v. Oklahoma* case of 1988, he appealed on the grounds that executing him for a crime he committed as a minor would constitute cruel and unusual punishment.

In a 5–4 opinion, the Supreme Court reversed the sentence, coming just short of declaring that no one under 16 could be

Mitigating Circumstances

Sandra Lockett was a recovering heroin addict from Akron, Ohio, with a minor criminal record. When she was 21, she visited New Jersey with her friend Joanne Baxter. While there, the women met Al Parker and Nathan Earl Dew. Parker and Dew went with the girls to their home in Akron, but the men did not have the money to buy transportation back to New Jersey. Dew offered to pawn, or sell, his ring, but the group's thoughts turned instead to robbing a pawn shop with a gun Sandra's father kept in his basement.

Sandra knew the owner of the pawn shop personally, so she waited in the getaway car when the others attempted the robbery. Al Parker held the gun, which went off and killed the pawnbroker. Sandra hid the gun when she heard what had happened. Eventually, all the participants were apprehended and charged with murder.

To avoid the death penalty, Parker—who had his hand on the trigger—took a plea bargain so that he would testify against the others. Lockett was also offered a plea bargain, and she turned it down three times.

The jury was instructed that "if the conspired robbery and the manner of its accomplishment would be reasonably likely to produce death, each plotter is equally guilty."[1] Lockett was convicted. The state of Ohio limited the "mitigating circumstances" her lawyer could present at sentencing, and Sandra's heroin addiction, her relatively minor criminal record, and her dismay at the unexpected death of the pawnbroker could not be considered.

The Supreme Court reversed her sentence, and in its decision eliminated any limitations on testimony that can be introduced as mitigating the circumstances of a capital crime.

1. *Lockett v. Ohio*, 438 U.S. 586 (1978). supreme.justia.com/us/438/586/case.html

executed. In effect, the Thompson case ended the execution of anyone under the age of 16. In 2005, the case of *Roper v. Simmons* extended the protection of juveniles from the death penalty to all who were under the age of 18 at the time the crime was committed.

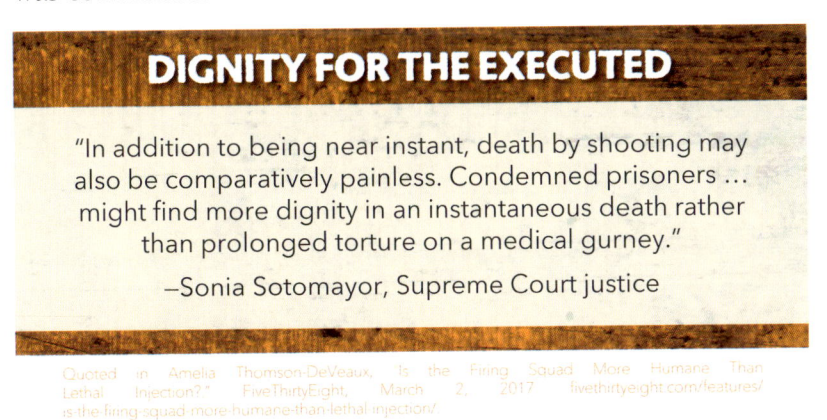

> **DIGNITY FOR THE EXECUTED**
>
> "In addition to being near instant, death by shooting may also be comparatively painless. Condemned prisoners ... might find more dignity in an instantaneous death rather than prolonged torture on a medical gurney."
>
> —Sonia Sotomayor, Supreme Court justice
>
> Quoted in Amelia Thomson-DeVeaux, "Is the Firing Squad More Humane Than Lethal Injection?," FiveThirtyEight, March 2, 2017. fivethirtyeight.com/features/is-the-firing-squad-more-humane-than-lethal-injection/.

Intellectual Disabilities of the Accused

John Paul Penry, arrested for the rape and murder of a woman in Texas, had a competency hearing before his trial that revealed that he was intellectually disabled, with the intellectual abilities of a six-and-a-half-year-old child. A psychologist described his social abilities as that of a nine- or ten-year-old. Despite these findings, the jury at that hearing found him competent to stand trial.

During *Penry v. Lynaugh* in 1989, Penry's lawyers claimed that he was incapable of learning and could not distinguish right from wrong. The prosecution introduced testimony from experts who said that Penry did know right from wrong but had an antisocial personality disorder. The jury sided with the prosecution and convicted him of murder; during the penalty phase of the trial, he was sentenced to death.

The laws in Texas did not provide for the central role of Penry's intellectual disability as a mitigating factor in his sentencing. Penry's lawyers brought this up on appeal, along with the claim that execution of the intellectually disabled would constitute cruel and unusual punishment.

The Supreme Court overturned Penry's conviction and instructed the state of Texas to change its sentencing procedures so that intellectual disabilities would be given full weight as a mitigating factor. However, the Court refused to bar execution categorically for the intellectually disabled, noting that the abilities of intellectually disabled people vary greatly, and each case must be examined separately.

In 2002, this decision was reversed in *Atkins v. Virginia*, when the Supreme Court disallowed executions of people with intellectual disabilities. Daryl Renard Atkins, who had an IQ of less than 70, had never lived on his own or held a job. The decision in this case was written by Justice Stevens: "We are not persuaded that the execution of [intellectually disabled] criminals will measurably advance the deterrent or the retributive purpose of the death penalty."[30]

Victim Impact Testimonies

Pervis Tyrone Payne was accused of attacking a 28-year-old mother of two young children. The woman and one of the children died. In the 1991 case of *Payne v. Tennessee*, the prosecution presented a victim impact statement describing the pain and suffering of the surviving child. The defendant appealed on the grounds that this kind of statement was prejudicial and violated the defendant's rights. Former cases had banned victim impact testimony, but this time, the Supreme Court affirmed its legality. This decision was seen as part of the growth of a victims' rights movement throughout the United States and as support for the pro-death penalty cause.

Herrera v. Collins, 1993

Leonel Herrera was convicted of killing two police officers in Texas. Two eyewitnesses, one a victim who subsequently died, testified that Herrera was the murderer. Herrera received the death penalty and began a series of appeals, the first of which claimed that the eyewitnesses were unreliable. This appeal was turned down by the Texas Court of Appeals, and the U.S. Supreme Court refused to review the case.

Herrera's next appeal came much later. He claimed that his own brother told Herrera's lawyer and son that he, not Herrera, had pulled the trigger and killed the policemen. However, Herrera's brother died before the appeal was filed. The Texas appeals court threw out the case, because during the original trial this evidence had not been introduced.

State and federal courts frequently hear cases that challenge standing capital punishment rulings.

Herrera then appealed to the Supreme Court in 1992. The Court had to consider whether the federal courts were obligated to hear appeals in death row cases on the basis of innocence, even if the grounds of innocence appear many years after the trial. In 1993, the Supreme Court decided 6–3 against Herrera, noting that his witnesses were no longer around to be cross-examined. The issue of the lapse of time was critical. The Court was saying that appeals such as Herrera's could go on forever, and at some point, legal closure is necessary.

Rights for Victims and Their Families

In recent years, the public has become more aware of the suffering caused by crime, especially murder, through television shows hosted by John Walsh (*America's Most Wanted*), Nancy Grace, and others. Walsh's son and Grace's fiancé were both murder victims.

The victims' rights movement seeks to ensure the rights of victims' families to be present and to be heard in all legal proceedings of the case, including plea bargaining and parole hearings, and to be notified if the criminal escapes from prison. It also calls for financial benefits and human services to be given by the government to victims. Most significantly for the death penalty issue, victims' rights advocates call for tougher sentences for criminals and for increasing the use of the death penalty in murder cases.

Supporters of victims' rights legislation cross political parties and philosophies. Some states have adopted a victims' rights platform into their constitutions. The U.S.

Ring v. Arizona: Who Should Decide a Death Sentence?

Timothy Ring and two accomplices robbed an armored car of $562,000 and shot the driver to death. Under Arizona's felony murder law, the jury convicted Ring of first-degree murder, but the full evidence necessary to sentence him to death was not presented at the jury trial. In 2002, at the sentencing hearing, Ring's partners testified against him, and the judge found that enough aggravating factors (especially the elaborate planning of the robbery and the cruel manner of the murder) applied to Ring's crime and qualified him for the death penalty.

The main issue in the Ring case was whether a jury, not simply the judge, should decide a death sentence. The majority opinion, written by Justice Ruth Bader Ginsburg, declared that the jury's deliberation was required and overturned Ring's sentence. Another court case in 2016, *Hurst v. Florida*, ruled to stop Florida executions because they went against the Ring

Congress has introduced the idea of adding victims' rights to the U.S. Constitution a number of times, beginning in 2003. The most recent House Joint Resolution was introduced on April 16, 2015.

The resolution states:

The following rights of a crime victim, being capable of protection without denying the constitutional rights of the accused, shall not be denied or abridged by the United States or any State. The crime victim shall have the rights to reasonable notice of, and shall not be excluded from, public proceedings relating to the offense, to be heard at any release, plea, sentencing, or other proceeding involving any right established by this article, to proceedings free from unreasonable delay, to reasonable notice of the release or escape of the accused, to due consideration of the crime victim's safety, dignity, and privacy, and to restitution. The crime victim or the crime victim's lawful representative has standing to assert and enforce these rights. Nothing in this article provides grounds for a new trial or any claim for damages.[1]

1. "H.J.Res 45–Proposing an Amendment to the Constitution of the United States to Protect the Rights of Crime Victims," U.S. Congress, accessed September 19, 2017. www.congress.gov.

judgment. Florida was instructed to ensure that all capital sentences are decided by a jury.

Debating the Method of Execution

In the 2008 case of *Baze v. Rees*, two inmates of Kentucky's death row, Ralph Baze and Thomas Bowling, appealed their death sentences on the grounds that lethal injection, the method of execution in the majority of American states, would violate the Eighth Amendment's prohibition of cruel and unusual punishment. Theirs was one of many cases that appealed on the same grounds, but it was the one granted a Supreme Court hearing.

As soon as certiorari (a hearing by the Supreme Court) was announced on September 26, 2007, executions were halted across the United States. The Supreme Court hears death penalty cases all the time, but this was the first case the Court had considered concerning the method of execution since *Wilkerson*

v. *Utah* in 1879, when it decided that executions by firing squad did not constitute cruel and unusual punishment.

Death by lethal injection involves the intravenous injection of three drugs, a lethal cocktail. The first drug is an anesthetic to put the convict to sleep; the second causes complete paralysis; the third brings about cardiac arrest. The possibility exists that the prisoner could regain consciousness during the final stage, during which the effect of the third injection, cardiac arrest, would cause great suffering.

This has happened in some instances, partly because trained physicians cannot carry out executions due to their professional ethics, and prison technicians have botched executions, causing extended and excruciating deaths. Nine states recognized these problems in the year before the Baze case and stopped their executions until a better method was found.

The Court heard oral arguments on January 7, 2008, and handed down its ruling on April 16. Seven justices rejected the challenge to lethal injection. Only two, Justices Ginsburg and David Souter, disagreed.

Kennedy v. Louisiana, 2008

Patrick Kennedy was convicted in Louisiana for the rape of his eight-year-old stepdaughter. The jury sentenced him to death for the rape. Six states, including Louisiana, include rape of a child as a crime that can be punishable by death sentence. In his appeal to the Supreme Court, Kennedy challenged that rape should not be punishable by death and constituted cruel and unusual punishment.

In a 5–4 split, the Supreme Court ruled that no crime other than murder should be punishable by death: "The court concludes that there is a distinction between intentional first-degree murder, on the one hand, and non-homicide crimes against individuals, even including child rape, on the other. The latter crimes may be devastating in their harm, as here, but in terms of moral depravity and of the injury to the person and to the public, they cannot compare to murder in their severity and irrevocability."[31]

Glossip v. Gross, 2015

After the *Baze v. Rees* ruling, drug companies stopped supplying states with the first drug for lethal injection due to their own concerns about being involved in capital punishment. The state of Oklahoma began to replace that drug with Midazolam, an unproven anesthetic. Three prisoners sued the state, and the case was taken to the Supreme Court. The court ruled the Eighth Amendment requires prisoners prove that another method of capital punishment is available, and in Oklahoma, there was not one. They also ruled that it was the prisoner's duty, not the state's, to prove that the drug did not cause unconsciousness and instead provided a cruel death.

Midazolam continued to be used in lethal injection cases throughout the United States, despite some horrific executions where the condemned person was awake and shouting in pain. In January 2017, an Ohio federal court judge ruled the use of

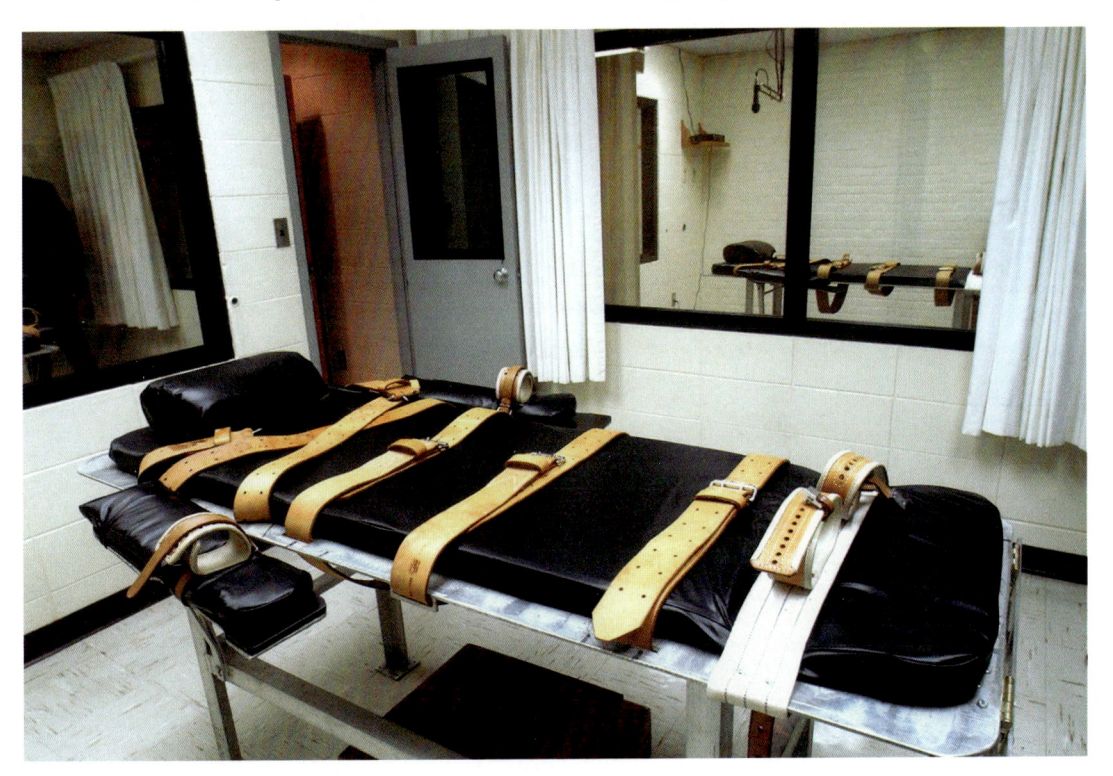

Shown here is the lethal injection execution room at the Mississippi State Penitentiary.

Midazolam in lethal injection was not humane enough. The court agreed with the plaintiffs that the drug could cause unnecessary suffering and pain.

Makers of Midazolam began to deny states access to the drug. Before their last supply of Midazolam expired in April 2017, the state of Arkansas scheduled the execution of eight death row inmates. Fresenius Kabi USA and West-Ward Pharmaceuticals Corp., the makers of potassium chloride and Midazolam, sued the state over illegal use of the drug. The manufacturers argued that they prohibit the use of their drugs for lethal injection and therefore the state of Arkansas must have purchased the drugs illegally. The state admitted to purchasing the drugs through a third party, but the court denied the suit by the pharmaceutical companies.

> **FINDING ALTERNATIVES FOR SHORTAGES OF LETHAL DRUGS**
>
> "I'll admit, it's more and more difficult to carry out the sentence of the death penalty ... We try to see if we can come up with another suitable formula of injection that will be humane, and then another lawsuit gets filed to say we can't do that either ... It is the law of the land—and until it's changed, until it's altered, you have to have a way to carry it out."
>
> —Andy Gipson, chairman of the Mississippi House Judiciary B Committee
>
> Quoted in Debbie Elliot, "States Find Other Execution Methods After Difficulties with Lethal Injection," NPR, April 6, 2017. www.npr.org/2017/04/06/522783564/states-find-other-execution-methods-after-difficulties-with-lethal-injection.

The Supreme Court denied an appeal by the prisoners to take up the case. Four were executed in the last few days of April. The final man executed, Kenneth Williams, was reported to have lurched and jerked for minutes after being injected with the drug.

A Global Look at the Death Penalty

According to Amnesty International, in 2016, 23 countries executed 1,032 individuals; this number excludes China, where the greatest number of executions has historically been carried out, though the exact number is unknown due to the secrecy of the government. Excluding China, 87 percent of executions occurred in 4 countries: Iran, Saudi Arabia, Pakistan, and Iraq. More than 3,000 people were sentenced to death in 55 countries, and more than 18,848 convicts live on death row around the globe. However, the majority of nations have outlawed capital punishment.

The General Assembly of the United Nations (UN) voted to approve a moratorium on the death penalty in 2016. It was the sixth time the UN had approved such a ban, and 117 countries voted for the ban, with only 40 voting against. One of the countries that voted no was the United States. Stefanie Amadeo, the deputy representative to the UN Economic and Social Council for the United States, said of the ban that "the ultimate decision regarding these issues must be addressed through the domestic democratic processes of individual Member States and be consistent with their obligations under international law."[32]

China's Secret Executions

China leads all other countries in use of the death penalty. Amnesty International reported in 2001 that 1,781 people were executed in China in 3 months of 2001. Death penalty advocates, along with opponents, have criticized the Chinese for the excessive and arbitrary nature of capital punishment in China. The Chinese have responded that executions have diminished greatly in number in the past few years. Amnesty International found public news reports of 931 people executed between 2014 and 2016, 85 of which are in the state database; however,

Most countries around the world oppose the death penalty.

any further information, including what the number of executions actually is, is unknown.

The death penalty was doled out to those convicted not only of murder or other violent crimes but also of offenses such as bribery, tax fraud, drug trafficking, selling harmful foodstuffs, and even stealing gasoline.

Some of the executions were blamed on an aggressive anti-crime campaign called Strike Hard. In Hunan Province, police claimed to have solved 3,000 cases in just 2 days in April. In Sichuan Province, the police said they arrested almost 20,000 people in 6 days. Most executions took place after sentencing rallies in public sports arenas and venues filled with spectators. On the way to the firing squads that would execute them, the convicts were paraded through the streets.

China continues to execute criminals by firing squads using assault rifles, but it has begun to also use lethal injection; in fact, protesters claim that lethal injection has been used more frequently to kill high officials, while ordinary people still face the firing squad.

China has been criticized for giving death penalty sentences to people who have committed nonviolent crimes.

The world's protests against capital punishment in China berate the country for the swift imposition of the death penalty, generally less than a year after sentencing, giving the prisoner little chance for appeal. Also, the imposition of the death penalty is uneven and unfair: When Strike Hard campaigns are staged by the central government, local officials respond with rapid trials and mass executions.

Iran's Mass Executions

Capital offenses in Iran include murder, adultery, terrorism, drug-related offenses, and sexual crimes, such as child sexual abuse and rape. Drug trafficking represents a high proportion of these offenses, as well as crimes against religion and execution for political purposes. Occasionally, the executions are carried out in public, and they are generally by hanging.

The Executioner Is Given the Punishment

The execution of Saddam Hussein by hanging occurred at dawn on the morning of December 30, 2006. The Iraqi dictator had received a lengthy trial, which ended in conviction for his role in the 1982 massacre of 148 Iraqis who were accused of plotting an assassination attempt against him. The White House statement by President George W. Bush said, "Fair trials were unimaginable under Saddam Hussein's tyrannical rule … It is a testament to the Iraqi people's resolve to move forward after decades of oppression that, despite his terrible crimes against his own people, Saddam Hussein received a fair trial."[1]

A statue of Saddam Hussein was toppled in Baghdad, Iraq, in 2003.

1. Quoted in Aneesh Raman, Arwa Damon, Ryan Chilcote, Sam Dagher, Jomana Karadsheh, and Ed Henry, "Hussein Executed with 'Fear in His Face,'" CNN, December 30, 2006. www.cnn.com/2006/WORLD/meast/12/29/hussein/index.html.

In August 2016, Iran held a mass execution of Sunni men. These 20 men were executed for practicing what the government saw as the "wrong" type of Islamic traditions, as the main government in Iran is of the Shi'a Islamic tradition. Religious minorities are targeted by the Iranian government. Other minorities, including LGBT+ individuals, are also punished with death sentences.

According to Amnesty International, Iran executed 567 people in 2016: "The authorities heavily suppressed the rights to freedom of expression, association, peaceful assembly and religious belief, arresting and imprisoning peaceful critics and others after grossly unfair trials before Revolutionary Courts. Torture and other ill-treatment of detainees remained common and widespread."[33]

Despite agreeing to follow international standards, Iran continues to execute people for non-violent crimes, including drug offenses. In 2013, Iran changed its penal code, on request of the UN Committee on the Rights of the Child, to allow retrials to those under age 18 on death row. Despite these promises, Iran continues to execute young men and women while juveniles. As of 2017, at least 90 people on death row in Iran are under age 18.

Saudi Arabia: Executing Juveniles

Saudi Arabia often uses beheading to carry out death sentences. On January 2, 2016, there were 47 executions held in 12 locations around the country. Those executed were convicted of terrorism, including a top Shi'a representative, or cleric, who was arrested after a political protest. The opposite of Iran, Saudi Arabia is a majority Sunni country, and those who practice Shi'a Islam are persecuted. Shi'a protesters and dissidents are often sentenced to death. In 2017, this sentence was given to 14 people.

Confessions offered by prisoners are often coerced using torture. The court then uses these forced confessions to sentence people to death. Generally, a forced confession is not true; at a certain point, people will admit to anything that makes the torture stop.

Juveniles are not exempt from the death penalty. In 2012, Abdullah Hasan al-Zaher, who was 15 years old at the time, was arrested along with other protesters. He was beaten by prison guards until he confessed to crimes against the government. His confession was used to sentence him to death. Although the

Shown here is Saudi Arabia's Deera, or "Chop-Chop," Square, where public executions have taken place.

international community has spoken out against the execution of al-Zahar and other juveniles, he is still imprisoned, awaiting beheading. After execution, corpses are sometimes hung in public places to discourage crime.

Honor Killings in Pakistan

After a six-year moratorium, the death penalty was reinstated in Pakistan in 2014 for terrorism offenses. By 2015, the death penalty was reinstated for additional crimes, and 87 people were executed in 2016. Pakistan has the world's largest recorded death row, with more than 6,000 awaiting execution. The death sentence may be imposed for 27 different charges. These include the capital crimes commonly punished elsewhere, such as murder or rape, and also blasphemy, stripping a woman of her clothes in public, and sabotage of the railway system.

Death often comes to those who are accused of blasphemy before they face trial. Pakistan has seen a rise in extrajudicial killings—murders carried out by people outside the justice system. One of those killed was Mashal Khan, a journalism student. After a discussion about religion on his college campus, a mob formed accusing Khan of blasphemy. The mob broke into his room and dragged him out to the street, where they beat him to death.

Activists are shown here lighting candles for victims of honor killings, or killings in which the victim was thought to have committed a crime that brought shame to their family.

Bringing Back the Death Penalty

In 2017, a few countries began to discuss bringing back the death penalty. In Turkey, President Recep Tayyip Erdoğan called for a national referendum to bring back the death penalty, which he had abolished as prime minister in 2014. Member countries of the European Union (EU), including Germany and the Netherlands, prevented Turkish citizens living in the EU from voting on the referendum. The EU said that bringing back the death penalty would mean Turkey could never join the EU. All EU countries have abolished the death penalty.

In the Philippines, President Rodrigo Duterte increased extrajudicial killings, or executing criminals before they had faced a court of law. He expressed intentions to bring the death penalty back to the Philippines. "People in the Philippines no longer believe in the laws, because the fear is not there,"[1] he said. A bill passed by the House of Representatives in that country increased the crimes punishable by death to include theft, piracy, infanticide (killing infants), rape, murder, keeping drug dens, and destructive arson. It also reduced the age someone could receive a death sentence to nine years old. Before a Senate vote, thousands of Catholics across the country marched against the death penalty in May 2017. The death penalty had been eliminated in 2006 in this majority Catholic country just before then-President Gloria Arroyo met with Pope Benedict.

1. Quoted in Eleanor Ross, "Philippines Votes on Reinstating Death Penalty and Reducing Age of Criminal Responsibility to 9," *Newsweek*, March 10, 2017. www.newsweek.com/philippines-vote-bring-back-death-penalty-565340.

The *Daily Times* of Pakistan wrote in January 2007: "We have retained the death penalty, with a lot of other countries in the world, because we think it will deter the killers among us. But the record shows that death is no deterrence. The big hangings in Pakistan as elsewhere have actually aroused conflicting passions and negated the concept of deterrence."[34]

A number of Pakistanis, generally women, are victims of honor killings each year. Honor killings punish crimes that are said to bring shame upon a family. The victims of honor killings are murdered by their own family. In conservative societies, honor crimes can consist of such infractions as marriage without the parents' consent; in one extreme case, a man murdered his wife and daughters for leaving the home without permission.

THE UNITED NATIONS REPORT ON IRAQ'S DEATH PENALTY

"UNAMI has strongly advocated that implementing the death penalty has no measurable deterrent effect on levels of insurgent and terrorist violence or on the levels of civilian casualties. A simple consideration of the numbers of civilian casualties each year since 2008 shows that, as the numbers of those executed have increased, so, too, has the number of civilian casualties who die from the actions of terrorist and armed groups. Far from having a deterrent effect, it would seem that the implementation of the death penalty is merely reactive to increasing violence."

—United Nations Assistance Mission for Iraq (UNAMI) and Office of the High Commissioner for Human Rights, author team of *Report on the Death Penalty in Iraq*

UNAMI Human Rights Office and Office of the High Commissioner for Human Rights, *Report on the Death Penalty in Iraq*, Office of the High Commissioner for Human Rights, October 2014. www.ohchr.org/Documents/Countries/IQ/UNAMI_HRO_DP_1Oct2014.pdf.

Although outlawed by the government in 2016, these honor killings have continued; there were 1,100 reported honor killings in 2016, although authorities believe another 1,000 may have been unreported.

Iraq Brings Back Capital Punishment

For almost 25 years, Saddam Hussein's government in Iraq executed its enemies at will, along with common criminals. There were 114 crimes that could be punished by death. The accused often had no trials at all, or hasty trials in which they were given no adequate representation. No totals are available, but Amnesty International documented more than 800 executions in just three years, 1980 to 1983. Many victims were nonviolent political prisoners who were members of banned political parties, students, and even children. Sometimes, corpses were returned to their families for burial bearing evidence of torture.

Following the American invasion of Iraq, U.S. Administrator Paul Bremer suspended the death penalty to assure Iraqis that the terror of Hussein's regime was over. Iraqis felt that capital punishment was one of many ways Hussein's regime had oppressed them, but the death penalty was reinstated in May 2005 in an attempt to restore order to revolutionary chaos in the country and punish terrorists.

In 2017, 36 insurgents who were convicted of aiding in a terrorist group were executed. The men had allegedly participated in a 2014 killing of Shi'a military cadets at a training camp. The trials lasted a few hours, and confessions extracted under torture were used to convict the men. The Iraqi government claims that the return of the death penalty for terrorists works to deter additional attacks. Evidence points to the opposite: Since reinstatement of the death penalty in 2005, terrorist actions have increased dramatically in Iraq.

Most Iraqis welcomed the return of capital punishment. Three murderers tried in 2005 were members of the Ansa al-Sunna Army. As the judge prepared to sentence them, he asked the victims' families for statements, and they did not hesitate to say that they wanted the death penalty.

Singapore: Using Punishment as Deterrent

The city-state of Singapore has more than 5 million people and one of the lowest crime rates in the world. In 2011, there were only 16 murders, and in 2012, there were 80 days in which no crimes happened. Many Singaporean citizens and lawmakers believe the exemplary law and order in their country is reason enough to continue capital punishment and that it must be a deterrent to criminal behavior. However, others believe there are other deterrent factors at work, such as cultural values.

> ### AN UNCIVILIZED PENALTY
>
> "The Parliamentary Assembly of the Council of Europe reaffirms its complete opposition to capital punishment. The Assembly considers that the death penalty has no legitimate place in the penal systems of modern civilised societies, and that its application constitutes torture and inhuman or degrading punishment within the meaning of Article 3 of the European Convention on Human Rights."
>
> —Parliamentary Assembly of the Council of Europe, Resolution 1253

Council of Europe. *Official Report of Debates*. Strasbourg, France. 2001. p. 677.

African Nations and the Death Penalty

Many African nations have experienced political unrest during the past decades. The nation of Nigeria is an example of a country that retains the death penalty to deter terrorism and revolution.

The death penalty was abolished in Nigeria in 2010, but it was brought back in response to expanding terrorism threats. In 2013, four criminals convicted of armed robbery were hanged. As of 2017, more than 1,000 people waited on death row in Nigeria.

In response to the kidnappings and terrorist acts by the group Boko Haram, Nigeria has expanded its death penalty to cover kidnappings. The police and military have detained anyone suspected of belonging to or aiding Boko Haram. The prisoners, and sometimes citizens fleeing the violence, are held in unsanitary detention centers. Many have died in these camps. Médecins Sans Frontières, a humanitarian organization that is known in English as Doctors Without Borders, reported 1,200 bodies buried near a camp in Bama, Borno State.

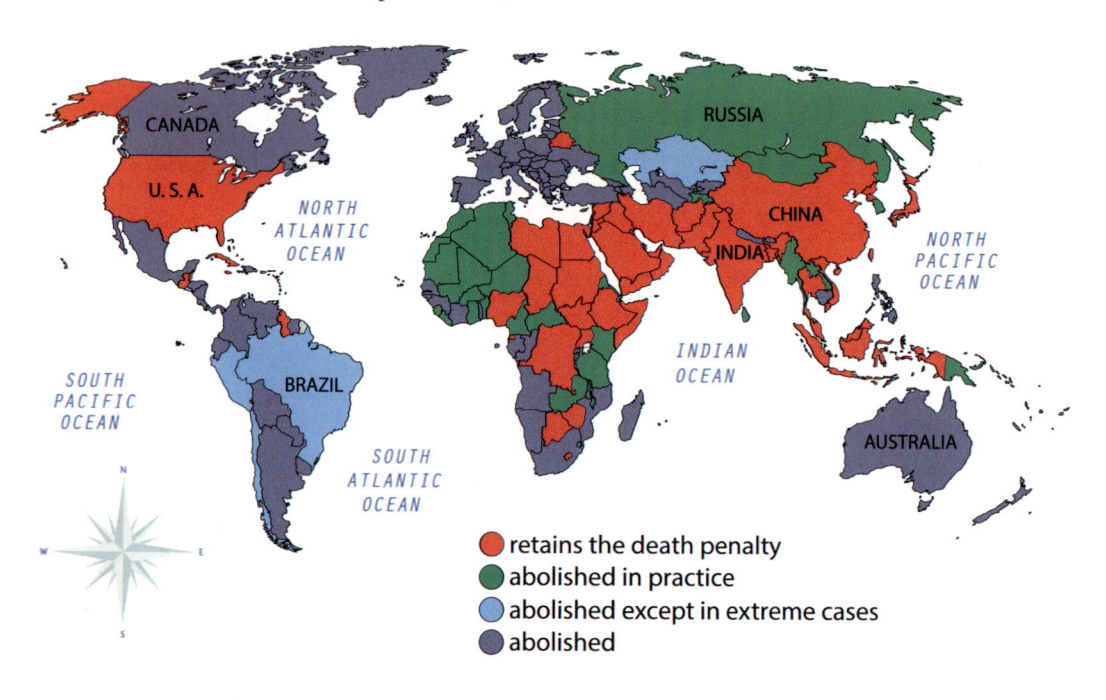

Shown here is a map of the death penalty status throughout the world as of 2017.

Although some African countries retain the death penalty, many more have abolished or revised their laws. The African Union (AU), a governing organization consisting of all 55 African countries, has begun to review the death penalty. In 2015, a commission recommended abolition of the death penalty and provided a draft protocol for other commissions within the AU to review. The document is still awaiting review by member states.

The European Union: Outlawing the Death Penalty

The European Union (EU) requires its member nations to abolish the death penalty, and the EU has established October 10 each year as the European and World Day against the Death Penalty. In 2016, the theme was anti-terror and the death penalty. The UN reiterated its statement that capital punishment for terrorism does not act as a deterrent but instead provides propaganda for increased terror attacks. In 2017, the theme was poverty and how those living in poverty are at greater risk of being given a death penalty sentence.

The world's nations continue to be split on the issue of capital punishment. For some governments, it is an outdated and inhumane practice, regardless of the methods or the rationale. Others, however, remain steadfast in their belief that capital punishment is a fair and reasonable way to punish criminals, deter crime, and protect society. Far from resolving itself, this ancient debate just seems to increase in complexity as human civilizations evolve, grow, and continually redefine their moral and legal expectations.

NOTES

Introduction: "An Eye for an Eye"

1. Quoted in Michael H. Reggio, "History of the Death Penalty," PBS *Frontline*, accessed September 13, 2017. www.pbs.org/wgbh/pages/frontline/shows/execution/readings/history.html.

Chapter 1: Sanctioning Punishment

2. Leviticus 24:17–20 (New International Version).
3. C.H.W. Johns, *Babylonian and Assyrian Laws, Contracts and Letters*. New York, NY: Charles Scriber's Sons, 1904, p. 64.
4. Quoted in S. Mendelsohn, *The Criminal Jurisprudence of the Ancient Hebrews*. Union, NJ: The Lawbook Exchange, Ltd., 2001, pp. 48–49.
5. Quoted in Edward Carpenter, *Cantuar: The Archbishops in their Office*. London, UK: Mowbray, 1997, p. 144.
6. Cesare Beccaria, "Of the Punishment of Death," Constitution Society, accessed September 14, 2017. www.constitution.org/cb/crim_pun28.htm.
7. Quoted in "Iran: Writer Facing Imminent Imprisonment for Story About Stoning," Amnesty International, October 6, 2016. www.amnesty.org/en/latest/news/2016/10/iran-writer-facing-imminent-imprisonment-for-story-about-stoning/.

Chapter 2: Support for the Death Penalty

8. Hashem Dezhbakhsh and Joanna M. Shepherd, "The Deterrent Effect of Capital Punishment: Evidence from a 'Judicial Experiment,'" *Economic Enquiry*, July 2006.

9. Dale O. Cloninger and Roberto Marchesini, "Execution Moratoriums, Commutations and Deterrence: The Case of Illinois," *Applied Economics*, May 20, 2006.

10. Committee on Law and Justice of the Division of Behavioral and Social Sciences and Education, "Deterrence and the Death Penalty," National Research Council, April 2012. deathpenaltyinfo.org/documents/NatResCouncil-Deterr.pdf.

11. Daniel S. Nagin, "Deterrence in the Twenty-first Century: A Review of the Evidence," Carnegie Mellon University, 2013. pdfs.semanticscholar.org/c788/48cc41cdc319033079c69c7cf1d3e80498b4.pdf.

12. Ronald Radosh and Joyce Milton, *The Rosenberg File: A Search for the Truth*. New Haven, CT: Yale University Press, 1982, p. 451.

13. Quoted in Gary P. Gershman, *Death Penalty on Trial*. Santa Barbara, CA: ABC-CLIO, 2005, p. 3.

14. Hugo Adam Bedau, "The Case Against the Death Penalty," American Civil Liberties Union, 2012. www.aclu.org/other/case-against-death-penalty.

15. Jolie McCullough, "Texas Death Penalty Juror Hopes to Change Law as Execution Looms," *The Texas Tribune*, March 28, 2017. www.texastribune.org/2017/03/28/texas-death-penalty-juror-hopes-change-law-execution-looms/.

Chapter 3: The Case Against the Death Penalty

16. Bedau, "The Case Against the Death Penalty."

17. Ernest van den Haag, "Capital Punishment Saves Innocent Lives," in *Does Capital Punishment Deter Crime?*, Roman Espejo, ed. Detroit, MI: Thomson Gale, 2003, p. 27.

18. "Causes of Wrongful Convictions," Death Penalty Information Center, accessed September 18, 2017. deathpenaltyinfo.org/causes-wrongful-convictions.

19. Bianca Jagger, "The Time Has Come to Say No to Death," *Huffington Post*, February 24, 2010. www.huffingtonpost.com/bianca-jagger/the-time-has-come-to-say_b_478388.html.

20. Quoted in Steve Mills and Maurice Possley, "Man Executed on Disproved Forensics," *Chicago Tribune*, December 9, 2004. www.chicagotribune.com/news/nationworld/chi-0412090169dec09-story.html.

21. Quoted in "Arbitrariness," Death Penalty Information Center, updated July 16, 2015. deathpenaltyinfo.org/article.php?did= 1328#Representation.

22. Quoted in Elaine Landau, *Teens and the Death Penalty*. Berkeley Heights, NJ: Enslow, 1992, pp. 47–48.

23. Robert J. Smith, Sophie Cull, and Zoë Robinson, "The Failure of Mitigation?," *Hastings Law Journal*, vol. 65, no. 1221, June 2014, p. 1256. www.hastingslawjournal.org/wp-content/uploads/Smith-65.5.pdf.

24. Billy Wayne Sinclair and Jodie Sinclair, *Capital Punishment: An Indictment by a Death-Row Survivor*. New York, NY: Arcade Publishing, 2009, e-book.

25. Quoted in "Race and the Death Penalty," Death Penalty Information Center, accessed September 19, 2017. www.deathpenaltyinfo.org/race-and-death-penalty.

26. Quoted in Kyle Cheek and Anthony Champagne, *Judicial Politics in Texas: Partisanship, Money, and Politics in State Courts*. New York, NY: Peter Lang Publishing, Inc., 2005, p. 132.

27. Quoted in Robert Barnes, "Supreme Court Says Race-Based Testimony Discriminated Against Black Death Death Row Inmate," *Washington Post*, February 22, 2017. www.washingtonpost.com/politics/courts_law/supreme-court-says-race-based-testimony-discriminated-against-death-row-black-inmate/2017/02/22/c7a1590a-f915-11e6-9845-576c69081518_story.html?utm_term=.45431b95b755.

28. Quoted in Erik Eckholm, "California Death Penalty, Struck Down Over Delays, Faces Next Test," *New York Times*, August 29, 2015. www.nytimes.com/2015/08/30/us/california-death-penalty-struck-down-over-delays-faces-next-test.html?_r=1.

Chapter 4: The Court's Rule on Capital Punishment

29. *McCleskey v. Kemp*, 481 U.S. 279 (1987). www.law.cornell.edu/supct/html/historics/USSC_CR_0481_0279_ZO.html.

30. *Atkins v. Virginia*, 536 U.S. 304 (2002). www.law.cornell.edu/supct/html/00-8452.ZO.html.

31. Quoted in "*Kennedy v. Louisiana*: Eighth Amendment Restrictions on the Death Penalty," Constitutional Law Reporter, accessed September 19, 2017. constitutionallawreporter.com/2015/11/09/kennedy-v-louisiana-eighth-amendment-restrictions-on-the-death-penalty/.

Chapter 5: A Global Look at the Death Penalty

32. Quoted in Lincoln Caplan, "The Growing Gap Between the U.S. and the International Anti-Death-Penalty Consensus," *The New Yorker*, December 31, 2016. www.newyorker.com/news/news-desk/the-growing-gap-between-the-u-s-and-the-international-anti-death-penalty-consensus.

33. "Iran 2016/2017," Amnesty International, accessed September 19, 2017. www.amnesty.org/en/countries/middle-east-and-north-africa/iran/report-iran/.

34. "Death Penalty and Increasing Crimes in Pakistan," Pakistan Press Foundation, January 30, 2007. www.pakistanpressfoundation.org/death-penalty-and-increasing-crime-in-pakistan/.

Discussion Questions

Chapter 1: Sanctioning Punishment

1. What were some of the early reasons for establishing capital punishment?
2. What crimes besides murder could be punished with capital punishment in early civilizations?
3. What role has religion played in the development of capital punishment?

Chapter 2: Support for the Death Penalty

1. Deterrence of future crimes is often cited as a reason for capital punishment. What did you take away from the studies quoted in this chapter? Does deterrence work?
2. How does the court system protect against false convictions?
3. Which of the arguments in favor of capital punishment seem the strongest to you? Explain your answer.

Chapter 3: The Case Against the Death Penalty

1. Why do opponents think juveniles should not be sentenced to death—even for terrible crimes?
2. How does race factor into death penalty sentencing?
3. Which of the arguments against capital punishment seem the strongest to you? Explain your answer.

Chapter 4: The Court's Rule on Capital Punishment

1. Why is the *Furman v. Georgia* case so important?
2. What rights are victims' families asking for during capital cases?
3. Explain how drug companies have influenced capital punishment.

Chapter 5: A Global Look at the Death Penalty

1. How does the death penalty in the United States differ from the death penalty in other countries?
2. What, other than terrorism, do you think contributes to countries bringing back the death penalty?
3. Do you think that the death penalty will ever be abolished everywhere in the world? Why or why not?

Organizations to Contact

American Civil Liberties Union (ACLU)
125 Broad St., 18th Floor
New York, NY 10004
(212) 549-2500
www.aclu.org

> The ACLU works to defend and preserve human rights and liberties guaranteed by the U.S. Constitution. Its website provides information on many topics concerning human rights, including the death penalty. The organization also has contact information for those needing legal assistance or a local ACLU affiliate.

Amnesty International USA
5 Penn Plaza, 16th Floor
New York, NY 10001
(212) 807-8400
www.amnestyusa.org

> Amnesty International is a worldwide movement of people who campaign for internationally recognized human rights for all. The organization tracks human rights abuses worldwide and reports on them; it has information on each country's use of the death penalty, which it opposes.

Equal Justice USA
81 Prospect St.
Brooklyn, NY 11201
(718) 801-8940
ejusa.org

> Equal Justice USA is an organization that focuses on both the accused and the victims. It works to prevent crime, help crime survivors, and support a fair and effective justice system.

The Innocence Project
40 Worth St., Suite 701
New York, NY 10013
(212) 364-5340
www.innocenceproject.org

> The Innocence Project works with prisoners to test DNA evidence and work toward overturning convictions. The organization works to reform the justice system to prevent wrongful future convictions and provide assistance to those still imprisoned through miscarriages of justice.

National Center for Victims of Crime
2000 M St. NW, Ste. 480
Washington, DC 20036
(202) 467-8700
www.ncvc.org

> The National Center for Victims of Crime is the nation's leading resource for crime victims, including the families of murder victims. Its website provides links to dozens of pro–death penalty articles and resources.

For More Information

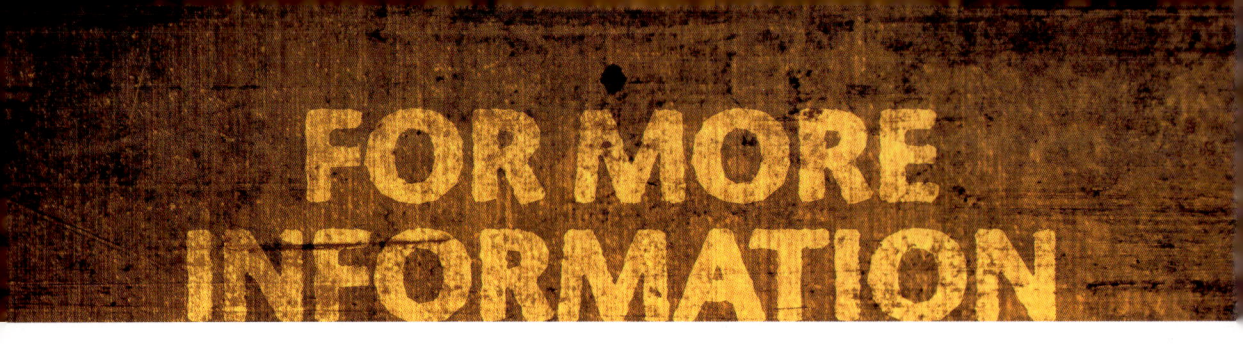

Books

Baumgartner, Frank, Marty Davidson, Kaneesha Johnson, Arvind Krishnamurthy, and Colin Wilson. *Deadly Justice; A Statistical Portrait of the Death Penalty*. Oxford, UK: Oxford University Press, 2017.
   Each chapter in this book uses evidence to examine a question surrounding the death penalty debate to decide whether the death penalty has worked.

Garrett, Brandon L. *Convicting the Innocent: Where Criminal Prosecutions Go Wrong*. Cambridge, MA: Harvard University Press, 2012.
   This book examines wrongful convictions and DNA exonerations, including exonerations for those who have been on death row.

Garrett, Brandon L. *End of its Rope: How Killing the Death Penalty Can Revive Criminal Justice*. Cambridge, MA: Harvard University Press, 2017.
   This book examines death row exonerations, race discrimination, wrongful convictions, and how they have all affected the death penalty.

Lane, Charles. *Stay of Execution: Saving the Death Penalty from Itself*. Lanham, MD: Rowman & Littlefield, 2010.
   This book is a discussion of the declining numbers of men and women being executed in the United States and the implications this has on crime, society, and the death penalty itself.

Wayne, Billy, and Jodie Sinclair. *Capital Punishment: An Indictment by a Death-Row Survivor*. New York, NY: Arcade Publishing, 2009.
   This book is the memoir of a man who was sentenced to death but had his sentence commuted by the *Furman v. Georgia* ruling in 1972. He went on to become a jailhouse lawyer fighting against the death penalty.

Websites

Death Penalty Information Center (DPIC)
deathpenaltyinfo.org
> The DPIC is the largest and most comprehensive death penalty website that includes information on current death row cases, state-by-state usage of the death penalty, and historical information.

The Execution
www.pbs.org/wgbh/pages/frontline/shows/execution/
> This PBS *Frontline* website has numerous articles and pages on the death penalty, including arguments for and against it, the history of the death penalty, and information on victims.

Students Against the Death Penalty
www.studentabolition.org
> Students Against the Death Penalty is an interactive, youth-oriented website with YouTube videos, blogs, and photos.

United Nations High Commissioner for Human Rights
www.ohchr.org/EN/Issues/DeathPenalty/Pages/DPIndex.aspx
> The High Commissioner's website provides international information on the death penalty, including statements from the UN.

U.S. Department of Justice, Bureau of Justice Statistics
www.bjs.gov/index.cfm?ty=tp&tid=18
> The Bureau of Justice Statistics publishes federal statistics on the death penalty in the United States, details of correctional populations, and other up-to-date information on executions and crime rates in the United States.

INDEX

A

Abbott, Jack Henry, 33–35
abolition, 21, 26, 65, 86
Age of Reason, 7, 47
Amadeo, Stefanie, 75
American Civil Liberties Union (ACLU), 33, 41
American Civil War, 21
Amnesty International, 10, 16, 25, 75, 79, 84
arguments against the death penalty, 57
arguments for capital punishment, 39
Atkins v. Virginia, 49, 68
atomic bombs, 31

B

Baldus, David, 64–65
Baze v. Rees, 10, 26, 59, 71–73
Beccaria, Cesare, 17, 19–20, 28, 41
Bethea, Rainey, 20
Bible, 9, 11, 19, 48
Blackwell, Earl, 55
blood price, 14
Bloodsworth, Kirk, 25–26
Boger, Jack, 54
Boko Haram, 85
botched executions, 57–58, 72
Bremer, Paul, 84
brutalization effect, 7
Buck v. Davis, 55

C

Cantu, Ruben, 43
Cathars, 16
Chessman, Caryl, 25
China, 10, 13, 75–77
Code of Hammurabi, 9, 11–13
Cold War, 24, 28, 31–32
Commission on the Fair Administration of Justice, 36
Confucius, 13
crucifixion, 6, 15
cruel and unusual punishment, 9–10, 26, 46, 48–49, 56–57, 59, 61–62, 65, 68, 71–72

D

Dead Man Walking, 25, 50
Death Penalty Information Center, 42, 64
deterrence, 20, 27, 30–33, 39, 42, 49, 56, 58, 68, 82–83, 85, 87
Dew, Nathan Earl, 66
DNA, 25–26, 39, 43
Dostoyevsky, Fyodor, 34
Draco's Code, 6, 13–14
Duterte, Rodrigo, 82

E

Edison, Thomas, 21
Eichmann, Adolf, 29
Eighth Amendment, 26, 30, 48–50, 56, 59, 71, 73
Enlightenment, 9, 19–20
Erdoğan, Recep Tayyip, 82
espionage, 31–32
European and World Day Against the Death Penalty, 86

F

Fair Punishment Project, 54
felony murders, 35, 70
first-degree murder, 7, 35, 63, 70
Ford v. Wainwright, 50

14th Amendment, 45, 61–62, 65
Franklin, Benjamin, 7, 19
French Revolution, 18
Furman v. Georgia, 9, 44, 61, 63

G

gas chamber, 8, 50, 58
Ginsburg, Ruth Bader, 45, 70, 72
Glossip v. Gross, 10, 59, 73
Gregg v. Georgia, 9, 45, 63–64
guillotine, 18

H

Hall v. Florida, 49
Harris County, Texas, 37, 45
Hastings Law Journal, 51
Henry VIII, 17
Herrera v. Collins, 68
honor killings, 80–81, 83
Huffington Post, 43
Hurst, Gerald, 44
Hurst v. Florida, 70
Hussein, Saddam, 78, 84
Hussites, 16

I

intellectually disabled, 49, 67–68
Iraee, Golrokh Ebrahimi, 25
Iran, 10, 24–25, 75, 77–79
Iraq, 75, 78, 83–84

J

Joan of Arc, 16–17
Jones v. Davis, 58
juveniles, 46, 48, 57, 67, 79–80

K

Kemmler, William, 22
Kendall, George, 7
Kennedy, John F., 41
Kennedy, Patrick, 72
Khan, Mashal, 81
Kinder, Brian, 55

L

law of parties, 40
Law of the Twelve Tables, 15
Lawson, David, 50
Legal Defense and Educational Fund (LDF), 53, 61, 64–65

lethal injection, 9–10, 26, 40, 43, 56, 59, 71–74, 76
Lewis, James, Jr., 46–47
lex Cornelia, 15
Lockett, Sandra, 66
Louis XVI, 18
lynching, 20–21

M

Marshall, Thurgood, 51
mass executions, 77–78
McCleskey v. Kemp, 64–65
Midazolam, 73–74
Middle Ages, 6, 16–17, 19
Myrdal, Gunnar, 52

N

National Research Council, 31
Nigeria, 85
Nixon, Richard, 63

P

Pakistan, 10, 75, 80–83
Parker, Al, 66
Payne v. Tennessee, 68
Penry v. Lynaugh, 49, 67
Pew Research Center, 26
Philippines, 82

Pilgrimage of Grace, 19
Pole, Reginald, 19
poverty, 37–38
Powell, Lewis, 65
Prejean, Sister Helen, 22, 50–51, 55
Progressive Era, 22

R

Reign of Terror, 18
reprieves, 34, 39–40
retribution, 11, 16, 27, 39, 49
Ring v. Arizona, 70
Roberts, John, 55
Robespierre, Maximilien, 18
Roof, Dylann, 41
Roper v. Simmons, 48, 67
Rosenberg, Ethel, 31–32
Rosenberg, Julius, 31–32
Russian Revolution, 7, 22

S

Sacco, Nicola, 9, 23
safeguards, 39
Salem witchcraft trials, 7
Sarat, Austin, 58
Saudi Arabia, 10, 24, 42, 75, 79–80
Scalia, Antonin, 30, 48, 62

Schick v. Reed, 40
Singapore, 42, 84–85
Smith, John, 34
Socrates, 14–15
Spanish Inquisition, 17
Stanford v. Kentucky, 48
Stewart, Potter, 44, 60
stoning, 11–12, 24–25
Strike Hard campaigns, 76–77

T

Texas Coalition to Abolish the Death Penalty, 37
de Torquemada, Tomás, 17
Trudell, Charles, 46–47

U

Unah, Isaac, 54
UN Committee on the Rights of the Child, 79
United Nations (UN), 10, 75, 83
U.S. Congress, 71

V

Vanzetti, Bartolomeo, 9, 23

W

Wainwright, Louie L., 50–51
Walsh, John, 70
Wilkerson v. Utah, 72
Williams, Dobie Gillis, 55
Willie, Robert Lee, 25
Willingham, Cameron Todd, 43–44
Witherspoon v. Illinois, 60
Woodson v. North Carolina, 63
Wuornos, Aileen, 25

Z

al-Zaher, Abdullah Hasan, 79

PICTURE CREDITS

Cover F. Carter Smith/Sygma via Getty Images; p. 8 travelview/Shutterstock.com; p. 12 Leah-Anne Thompson/Shutterstock.com; p. 13 jsp/Shutterstock.com; p. 15 JarektUploadBot/Wikimedia Commons; pp. 17, 32 Universal History Archive/Getty Images; p. 18 Nils Versemann/Shutterstock.com; p. 21 Everett Historical/Shutterstock.com; p. 27 Dukes/Shutterstock.com; pp. 29, 61 Bettmann/Contributor/Bettmann/Getty Images; p. 36 AVN Photo Lab/Shutterstock.com; p. 37 sirtravelalot/Shutterstock.com; p. 42 Dirk Ercken/Shutterstock.com; p. 47 sophie ELBAZ/Sygma via Getty Images; p. 51 Brooks Kraft LLC/Sygma via Getty Images; p. 57 Yeexin Richelle/Shutterstock.com; p. 60 Orhan Cam/Shutterstock.com; p. 69 zimmytws/Shutterstock.com; p. 73 AP Photo/Rogelio Solis, File; p. 76 Guru 3D/Shutterstock.com; p. 77 STR/AFP/Getty Images; p. 78 Gilles BASSIGNAC/Gamme-Rapho via Getty Images; p. 80 Andrew V Marcus/Shutterstock.com; p. 81 AAMIR QURESHI/AFP/Getty Images; p. 86 Ivsanmas/Shutterstock.com.

ABOUT THE AUTHOR

Allison Krumsiek is an author and poet living in Washington, D.C. She currently writes for a number of organizations, including nonprofits and the federal government, as well as other titles in Lucent's Hot Topics series. When she is not writing or editing, she can be found reading books or fearlessly defending her field hockey goal, but never at the same time.